Other books by Kendra E. Ardnek:

*The Ankulen*
*The Seven Drawers*
*The Worth of a King*
*A Twist of Adventure*

**The Rizkaland Legends**
*Water Princess, Fire Prince*
*Lady Dragon, Tela Du*
*Love and Memory*
*The Isle of Talking Beasts (Coming Soon!)*

**The Bookania Quests**
*Sew, It's a Quest*
*Do You Take This Quest?*
*My Kingdom for a Quest*
*Honor: A Quest In*
*Hair We Go Again*
*The Merchant of Menace*
*Snow Quest Like Home (Coming Soon!)*

**The Austen Fairy Tale**
*Rose Petals & Snowflakes*
*Crown & Cinder*
*Emmazel*
*Snowfield Palace (Coming Soon!)*

When Emma is trapped as Rapunzel

# Emmazel

The Austen Fairy Tales — 3

Kendra E. Ardnek

ISBN: 9798360268550

# Dedication

For Brielle. 'Cause I can.

# Who's Who?

Emmazel: Rapunzel / Emma Woodhouse
Night: Knightly
Father: Mr. Woodhouse
Heather: Harriet
Berry: Mr. Bates
Kendra Flaxseed: Jane Fairfax
Christian: Frank Churchill
Mr. E: Mr. Elton
Mrs. E: Mrs. Elton
Anna: Ann Weston

1

Despite having lived her whole life in a tower, Emmazel had made it to maturity with a reputation of being clever and accomplished. Too clever, if one asked her father. And too fond of love potions.

Thirty-two companions, she'd had during her tenure in the tower, and nearly every one of them was now married into the country's nobility. Anna was the latest, an older woman who had been a decided old maid. Emmazel had considered her an especial challenge but had still prevailed in the end.

"Emma! Emmazel, child, where are you?"

She sighed at her father's call, sending one last surge of magic into the coriander she was tending, and then she stood. He had just returned home and clearly wasn't happy with what he'd found.

"I'm in my garden, Father!" she shouted down the stairs. "It was such a beautiful day. I just *had* to do some gardening."

The winds swirled, and suddenly he stood beside her in the room. Her garden was the most remarkable room – for though she couldn't go outside herself, the roof was made of the clearest crystal, allowing light to pass through and her plants thrived.

"Emmazel, where is your companion?"

Emmazel blinked and glanced about herself, as though surprised that he should ask such a question. "Well, not here, obviously. Did you misplace her?"

"Emmazel, child, you are being meddlesome again, aren't you?"

"It was another lord, sir," she declared. "He'd been bothering us for weeks, convinced that I was here against my will, and I just *had* to do something about it."

"You used a love potion on the pair," piped up the black cat who lay sunning himself among her roses.

"Again, child?" Father twisted away, throwing up his hands in frustration, and the wind that followed him rustled through the room with particular agitation. A few of Emmazel's plants complained, but most were used to his outbursts. "I go to so much trouble to find companions for you, here in your tower, and all you do is trick the poor girls into falling in love with lords and dukes and running away with them."

Emmazel shook her head, kneeling to tend her plants. "Papa, you've forbidden me to leave this tower, so you can't possibly expect me to have run off with him in her place. What else was I to do?"

"Turn him away! Make it clear that neither one of you is a damsel in distress and that his services are unneeded and unwanted." Father shook his head in disappointment. "Love is not to be trifled with."

"And young men who have it in their heads that there's a helpless young maiden for them to rescue aren't to be trifled with, either," Emmazel countered. "You underestimate the power of love, Papa."

"You meddle with things you don't understand," said Father. "Stop herding these poor fellows to marriage with your potions."

"You do know that the entire reason that girls agree to come live with me is because I'll help them find a husband of rank?" Emmazel raised an eyebrow. "Night can attest! None would be so brazen to admit it outright when you're recruiting them, but most have said as much to me. And I make sure to let them know the risks of a love potion, and each is instructed to delay the marriage for at least the six months that it takes for a love potion to wear off. And I hear that most of my girls are quite happy with their lives since. Why, Lady Bellflower sent me a necklace just last month as a thank-you for my help. I assure you, I know what I'm about."

Father threw up his hands. "As always, you won't listen to me, thinking instead that you know best. Mark my words, dear Emmazel, and stop all this bothersome trouble before you regret it all."

Emmazel tilted her head to the side as she considered her father. How old and frail he looked these days! Perhaps she really ought to pay more attention to him, for it seemed unfair for a man to slip away this quickly, and he'd been strong and hale for as long as she could remember.

"I think," she said at length, "that you're out of sorts because it's dinnertime. Why don't we retreat to the kitchen? Anna didn't leave us without supper. You, too, Night. Come along!"

She scooped up the black cat and headed down the stairs, knowing that her father would follow. He would also continue his protests, despite the futility.

"You don't have to bother yourself, good lady," said Night, squirming in her arms. "I have four legs that work perfectly well, in case you didn't realize."

Emmazel laughed and hugged him closer. "But then you might get lost, and just think how distraught I'll be!"

~

They sat down around the table, and Emmazel passed around the night's dinner of vegetables and chicken. All were mindful of the empty chair.

Or, at least, Emmazel and her father were. Night hopped up to his seat and made himself quite comfortable, paying it no mind.

"There's no question about it; I'll just have to find another girl to stay with you." Father tsked and shook his head. "It's no good, leaving you here alone. No, you need a new companion, and I'll just have to find one entirely disinterested in marrying above her station."

"Good luck with that," said Emmazel. "There's no one in the land who wouldn't like to improve their lives, and marriage is the best way for a woman to do that. Why, even as content as *I* am, I might be tempted myself if Prince Christian were to stumble upon my tower and suit for my hand."

"Emma! Emmazel, child!" Father shook his head in distress. "Put such a thought from your mind! You have no need of anything outside the tower. And why would the prince have reason to visit you? I'm certain he's far too busy doing the things that princes do."

Emmazel just wiggled her eyebrows as she took a sip of her tea. "You're quite likely correct," she acquiesced. "Though, Anna's husband-to-be is the Duke of Westbrook, Prince Christian's own cousin. So you might never know."

Father's frown grew.

"Perhaps, sir, you ought not to worry so much about what Emma does with the girls," Night suggested. "A fool she might be; at least it keeps her in the tower."

Father harumphed. "The tower is for her own good, as she well knows. Emmazel is too delicate a flower for the outside world, and I don't know if my nerves could take it, should she ever leave."

Emmazel reached over and patted her father's hand to comfort him. "And with the stories you tell, I shudder at such exposure. So put your mind quite at ease, Papa, and know that I have no intention of leaving the home you built for me.

So long as he lived, Emmazel could never leave her father. Not when he sat there before her, so frail and old. She was all he had, and she couldn't leave him adrift.

"You're a good daughter," said Night. "A veritable model of perfection. Isn't that right, sir?"

Emmazel sat up straighter, simpering under the praise, even if she had no idea how serious the cat was. He *did* love to tease her.

"She has flaws enough – which she would do well to remember," said Father. "Don't go filling her head with idle praise, cat."

"Idle? Never!" Night licked his paw as though offended. "But if I puff up her head enough, it might well actually be able to match that braid of hers."

Emmazel gave the cat an offended huff. She was quite proud of her golden braid, which had never been cut and was nearly twice as long as she was tall, despite her height. She had an idea that the length would be unmanageable if she had to move about outside, but in the tower, it was nothing to worry over. Brushing and braiding it kept her occupied for a good hour each day, besides, and she prided herself on always staying busy despite her confinement.

"She doesn't need your help with that," said Father, shaking his head. "Now, I don't want any of that cake, sitting there under the towel, so I am off to bed. If you want my advice, you would leave that thing alone yourself, my dear. It's far too rich for this late in the evening. But, of course, you won't listen to me – ah, Night, is this how children are these days? Always thinking they know best."

Night paused, a curious expression crossing his face as he sat up straight. "I wouldn't know, but it certainly seems true of your daughter, sir. I think it comes of her confinement in this tower. It gives her ideas that she knows everything about the world."

Father stared at Emmazel for a long moment, then turned away. "There's nothing to be done about that. Alas." With that, he disappeared from the room, taking his unruly winds with him.

Emmazel narrowed her gaze on Night. "You infuriating cat! You know better than to upset him like that!"

"And so do you, yet you still persist in making your love potions."

"It's hardly my fault that men are so obsessed with rescuing maidens trapped in towers." Emmazel shook her head. "Neither is it my fault that they are so easily swayed *by* a potion. Why, it's really only a precaution to keep them from fixating on me."

"As you've said."

"And I'm quite aware that I don't know everything – how can I when there's a whole world out there that I have never experienced for myself? But I do know what I know, and you can't take *that* away from me, you disagreeable cat!"

"So you say." Night was done eating, so he jumped down from the table. "Now, you seem to be on your own to clean up tonight. Such a pity. I'd offer to help, but I lack hands."

Emmazel pursed her lips as she stared after Night. Shaking herself, she wrapped up the cake and put it away. It had been meant as a peace offering for her father, and since that had failed – well, it was better off as breakfast tomorrow.

2 "Emmazel! Emmazel, let down the ladder – I have the new girl for you. Don't keep her waiting. She's a skittish young thing, and I would hate for her to run."

Emmazel rushed to the window, leaning out to observe her newest companion. It was hard to see from her height of sixty feet from the ground, but the yellow braids looked promising.

Nodding in satisfaction, Emmazel reached for the vines that framed her window, giving a silent order. The vines trembled and then unfurled, reaching to the ground as they formed a stepladder for the girl to climb.

When a moment passed, and the girl just stared, frozen, Emmazel gave another order. One vine swung free and wrapped around the girl's shoulders and under her arms.

The girl was adorably surprised, but Father seemed able to assure her quickly enough, and she finally began to climb. Up and up she went, the vine wrapped around her retracting with as she climbed, so she wouldn't fall even if she slipped. The girl's confidence grew with each step she took, and soon Emmazel was pulling her through the window.

"Why, aren't you charming!" Emmazel cried, sizing the girl up.

And she was, in a quaint sort of way. She was small but sturdy, her red-gold hair was bound in practical braids, and a smattering of freckles spread across her pert nose.

"What's your name, dear?"

The girl was catching her breath, but her blue-green eyes went wide at Emmazel's question, and she dropped into a deep curtsey. "Heather, ma'am."

"Heather! A charming name, too." Emmazel smiled even wider to reassure her new companion. "And I'm Emmazel, though I suspect my father already told you as much. Now, if you're here to be my companion, there's no need for that hesitation. Chin up – you're going to be my friend, not my servant. Remember that, Heather."

Yes, her father had undoubtedly found a timid one this time. But it was all just the better challenge and greater triumph at the end of it all.

"Yes, ma'am, of course." Heather bobbed into another curtsy, and Emmazel bit her tongue. A greater challenge indeed!

Taking a breath, Emmazel glanced out the window and nodded in satisfaction as she saw that her father had left them alone. He would be back again tonight, but for now, he was busy, and she and Heather were free to acquaint themselves the way she liked.

"Why don't you come down to the kitchen with me," she suggested, smiling wider to reassure her new friend. "We can get to know one another over cake – how does that sound?"

Heather nodded, wide-eyed and wordless, and followed Emmazel down the stairs to the kitchen level of the tower.

"So, tell me about yourself," Emmazel instructed, putting a slice of cake before the girl. "What is your family, how old are you, and what are your hopes and dreams in life?"

Heather fidgeted with her fork, her lips twisted in a hesitant smile, and a blush spread across her freckled nose. Father had really meant it when he set out to find the most unassuming girl in existence.

Ah, how Emmazel loved a challenge! No companion of hers could stay common for long.

Half of Heather's cake was gone before she spoke. "I don't know anything about my parents. I was left on the blacksmith's doorstep as a baby and was raised with their children, though they always made sure to remind me that I wasn't *theirs*."

Emmazel clucked her tongue, shaking her head. "You dear thing! Some people have no sense of compassion!"

The girl pulled back and gave a sheepish shrug. "They didn't have to take me in, but they did."

"Austere forbid that they leave you to the elements and wildlife! You were a baby!"

Heather shrugged again, her blush deepening. "They could have handed me off. I'm grateful to them, and that's enough."

Emmazel did *not* think that was enough but realized that it was a battle that wouldn't be won all at once.

"Do you ever wonder about your parents? Your *real* parents, that is. Who were they, and why did they have to give you up? It must have been *such* a tragedy!"

Heather's eyes darkened as she ate the last few bites of cake. "I … choose to not think about it, when possible. And most of the time, it is possible, and I have only myself to worry about."

Ah! Such a dull imagination was not to be tolerated!

Emmazel leaned back in her seat, effecting a dreamy expression. "With features as fine as yours, I can't imagine that your blood could be common – not purely common, at least. What if your parents were star-crossed lovers, the world against them, and you were stolen from your mother's arms as they were ripped apart!"

Heather's nose wrinkled in thought before she dismissed it with another shrug. "Or they could have been peasants who couldn't afford to feed another mouth, so they pawned me off on someone they thought was more advantaged."

"Perhaps, but that is such a gloomy thought – I like to imagine the *best* possible scenario."

Heather pulled back in visible distress. "I don't consider the thought that my parents could be separated and heartbroken to be the *best possible* scenario."

Emmazel waved her hand. "Oh, I'm sure they've found each other, by now, but had no idea where to find you – they might not even know that you still live!" She punctuated with a sigh. "Or perhaps your mother died in childbirth, your father couldn't be found, and so the poor midwife left you on the doorstep of a family she thought could care for you. The possibilities really are endless."

"Endlessly awful! How is that at all better?" Heather stood and tugged on one of her braids.

"Ah, I see you have no inclination for the game." Emmazel shook her head as she stood. "No matter – should we make guesses about my own mother instead?"

Heather paused and blinked. "Your mother?"

"I don't know a thing about her, and I don't remember her," Emmazel explained. "So I like to make up stories and guess at what sort of woman she was and what happened to her. It keeps me from boredom, even if I can gain no true answers from it."

"Doesn't your father tell you about her?" asked Heather.

Emmazel shook her head. "I don't dare even bring her up with him, for it distresses him greatly. So I know it must have been a true tragedy."

"I'm so sorry."

"It's part of life," said Emmazel, reaching over to squeeze Heather's hand. "Night says I shouldn't even think about her, but she was my mother. I think I owe it to her to keep her alive in my mind."

Heather nodded. "I suppose so. Who is Night?"

Emmazel tilted her head to the side, considering. "A friend of mine. We'll see how long it takes for him to introduce himself. You know, I've had companions that he never spoke to once, the insufferable creature."

Heather's nose wrinkled in an adorable frown. "Oh."

"If and when he does decide to speak to you, just know that it's a rare honor."

"All right. I will."

Emmazel laughed at the girl's simplistic eagerness, took the plate and fork from her, and set them in the sink to wash later.

"Come," she said. "I'll show you your duties as my

companion while you tell me what you want out of life."

The girl trotted after Emmazel, and it only took a little more coaxing before her tongue loosened and she chattered about her … *modest* ambition.

Heather, above all else, wanted to be useful. Emmazel tried hard to not judge that as a tragedy of the *worst* kind, but it was somewhere to begin. The girl's whole life, people had only ever wanted her for her usefulness, and so that was all she knew.

The blacksmith's family had turned Heather out a year before, having no more need of her now that their youngest son was old enough to be apprenticed and the three daughters could do her chores. She'd spent the time since with a family of farmers. They'd been happy to have an extra set of hands, but she'd never quite felt that there was room for her in the tiny house.

"That was why I was glad of the opportunity that your father gave me," Heather explained. "You have plenty of space in this tower, and I won't be a burden."

Emmazel clucked her tongue and patted Heather's shoulder. "You aren't a burden at all, so put all of your worries out of your mind. I'm infinitely grateful to have you here with me, Heather, and I hope to soon count you among my dearest friends."

~

"Emmazel, Emmazel! Let down your hair!"

Emmazel reluctantly set her book to the side and went to the window to roll her eyes at the black cat below. "There are vines for you to climb, Night," she shouted down at him. "You know that. You don't have to be a pest every time you want to enter the tower."

"Ah, but your hair would make such a lovely ladder if you should put it to such a use. Might finally give you a reason to walk around with so much attached to your head."

Emmazel pursed her lips as the cat leapt up onto the vines and bounded from one to another. "The new girl is in the kitchen if you'd like to go say hello to her," she said, before retreating back to her chair to resume reading. "Or just stare at her and meow, if that's what you would prefer."

The cat didn't answer as he appeared in the window and then disappeared down the stairs to the kitchen.

Emmazel kept her gaze on her book but hardly read a word until Night returned and hopped up on the chair across from her.

"She's a sweet girl; don't ruin her, Emmazel."

Emmazel threw down the book with an indignant huff. "Ruin her!" she cried. "You infuriating cat! I will do nothing of the sort – if ever a girl deserved elevation and self-confidence, it's her."

Night gave a huff of his own. "What she doesn't deserve is meddling."

"You have so little faith in me!" Emmazel shook her head. "Night, all I want is to give her the life she deserves after all of the hardships she's faced."

Night whipped his tail around himself and licked a paw as he seemed to gather his thoughts. "Not everyone has shoulders strong enough to support a head puffed up with self-importance," he finally stated. "You can pull the look off, but I fear it would ruin her."

"Well!" Emmazel paused as she tried to determine if Knight had slid a compliment into that statement. She knew she shouldn't care so much about it, but one needed ways to pass the time.

"She could use some self-confidence," Night mused, "and a true friend, but you have a reputation, Emmazel. Heather is sweet and unassuming, with a kind and loving heart. Teach her to value herself, and I agree that she needs some confidence, but don't ruin her."

Emmazel frowned as she stared down the stairs toward the kitchen. "Do you really trust me so little, Night? We've known each other for so long – I thought us friends!"

"Good friends are never afraid to warn each other before they make a mistake," said Night.

"Is that so?" Emmazel shut the book, stood, and scooped

up the cat, tucking him under her arm. "Well, I thought you knew what a mistake it is to tell me what to do with my girls. I *will* see her life bettered, no matter how much you protest."

Night gave a disgruntled growl but could do nothing about his position. Emmazel held him too tightly.

"Now," she continued, "I know you love to torment me, but we have a guest today, so do be on your best behavior."

"When am I otherwise, dear Emmazel?"

"Often." And with that, Emmazel marched down the steps to see how Heather was doing.

"Is he your cat?" asked Heather, smiling as she saw them. "He's in the village all the time. I've never thought he was a stray, not with how well taken care of he is, but I never imagined that he belonged to *you*."

Emmazel arched an eyebrow as she sat Night down in a chair. "'Belongs to' are strong words for a cat," she answered. "But he likes to hang around here most of the time. I think he likes the way we feed him."

Heather's nose wrinkled as she nodded. "That makes sense. He's a nice cat. I'm glad he has a home."

Night gave no comment. Clearly, he wasn't yet ready to let Heather hear him, and far be it from Emmazel to ruin his fun. She knew that talking cats weren't the norm, and he kept silent for the same reason she stayed in the tower. Safety.

"How is supper coming? Our friend seems to be getting hungry." Emmazel scratched Night behind the ears. "Do you need my help with anything?"

Heather shook her head. "Oh, no! I have it all under control, don't you worry! I—"

"You're here to be my companion, not my servant. I've finished with my garden for the day and have cleaned upstairs, so now I'm here to help with supper. No buts!"

Besides, this kept Night from criticizing Emmazel's choices, since he was determined to stay silent around Heather.

*3* Apart from her father, Night, and her steady stream of companions and their princes, Emmazel had one other frequent visitor, Berry, a fairy who worked for the Flaxseeds, the most influential family in the neighboring village of Hightower. Berry was an older fairy, having served the family for some seven years – an impressive feat, given that fairies lived only a decade at most – and she loved to talk.

Oh, how she loved to talk.

Emmazel didn't know how to tell Berry to stay away, not when the fairy came to help keep Emmazel's loneliness at bay. Her loneliness wasn't a *terrible* problem, but Emmazel still couldn't afford pickiness when it came to friends.

She suspected the same was true for Berry, but she didn't know *that* much about the outside world.

Regardless, Berry was there every third morning, just bursting with gossip from the Flaxseed household.

"A letter from Miss Kendra today!" Berry announced this morning. "I know how you love those, Miss Emmazel."

No, Emmazel did *not* love Kendra Flaxseed's letters, but Berry had it fixed in her mind that Kendra and Emmazel were of an age and, therefore, *ought* to be great friends. The truth of the matter was, though Emmazel couldn't say how old she herself was, she remembered when Kendra was but a babe. She'd watched Kendra grow up.

Grow up free to explore the world, speak to everyone, and accept the opportunity to go to the capital to live as a lady-in-waiting for Lady Camilla.

But she was a boring, ordinary girl and far too perfect for Emmazel's tastes. Nothing exciting about her, really. No, they weren't friends and never would be.

"I have to tend my garden," Emmazel said. "You'll have to read it to me while I work."

"Of course, yes!" cried Berry, flying after Emmazel as she ascended the tower steps to the rooftop garden.

If she was going to listen to Berry praising Kendra's many, *many* dull accomplishments, then Emmazel would need all of the fortitude she could get – and nothing compared to gardening for strengthening one's nerves.

"They've had the wedding – that's what this letter is all about," Berry chattered away as Emmazel knelt before her flowerpots. "Lady Camilla has married Lord Dickon, and it was just as glorious as you could imagine!"

"Marriages among the nobility generally are," Emmazel commented, chiding a weed and pulling it from the soil. These weeds really needed to learn their place, and it was always the greatest mystery to her how they found their way to the top of her tower.

"Of course, of course, you would know all about that, what with the way that all of your companions seem to find noble husbands."

"Precisely," said Emmazel.

"Ah, but you've never been able to attend a single one of those weddings, which is such a shame," Berry continued, flittering around Emmazel's head. "But Kendra has described *this* one in *such* detail, and so I shall share all of it."

"How generous."

"Oh, yes, I thought so myself." Berry clapped her hands together and sat down on a rose. "And it was a splendid wedding, as I already said. The chapel was filled with roses, and Lady Camilla wore a dress in the loveliest shade of blush, stitched with silver thread. Oh, and the music – they had a full orchestra as she walked down the aisle, just as beautiful as you can imagine! And the food! The banquet was twelve courses and no less!"

"It sounds glorious," said Heather from the steps.

Emmazel twisted around to stare at her with a raised eyebrow, and she drew back with a sheepish wince.

"I'm sorry, I was bringing you the breakfast scraps, as you requested. I didn't mean to eavesdrop, but I didn't realize you had a guest."

Emmazel eased into a smile to reassure her companion. "Oh, you're quite all right. This is Berry – she can fly, and she likes to visit to tell me everything that's happening outside. I'm quite grateful to her. She's telling me all about the letter that Kendra Flaxseed has sent about a noble wedding."

"Yes, I gathered it was a wedding." Heather gave a long sigh. "And it sounds amazing. I've attended weddings, but none so grand as that."

"Of course not," said Emmazel. "Things are always more extravagant for the nobility and rich. They have more money to spend, after all. Appearances to maintain."

"Of course," said Heather.

Emmazel gave a sigh. "Of course, the wedding only belongs to the *lady who* Kendra serves. Kendra remains nothing but a companion, herself."

Heather's nose wrinkled in confusion as she clearly failed to comprehend Emmazel's meaning.

"Perhaps not, but it's still a great honor to *be* a lady-in-waiting," Berry countered. Such a loyal thing. "Kendra has done quite well for herself. There's no mistaking that. And she didn't even *need* to fall in love to do it."

Emmazel refrained from rolling her eyes. "Is falling in love *such* a terrible fate?"

"Well, perhaps it isn't," said Berry. "If you do it properly, it can make you quite happy, I will agree there, but Kendra says it's a dreadful shame that women must depend on men and marriage if they want to improve their lives."

Emmazel focused on encouraging the growth of a sickly

patch of thyme as she gathered her response. Because she didn't *disagree* with the sentiment – but far be it from her to agree with Kendra Flaxseed.

"It's not the only way – it's just the most fun," she said. "Men must labor and toil, but if she catches the right man's eye, a pretty girl could have the world handed to her in a moment. And if she loves him back – well! I don't believe for a moment that a woman *depends* on a man."

"Well, that's true enough, but you can't fault Kendra for wanting to do things her own way." Berry was flittering about again.

"I suppose we can't," said Emmazel.

But Kendra didn't have to be so high-minded about it. As though she were so much better than other women for wanting to get ahead by her own efforts and not relying on marriage. It was truly horrifying.

"Well, I think that's everything I came to tell you," Berry announced. "And the Flaxseeds have a whole *list* of chores for me to attend to today, so I really must be off!"

And with that, the fairy disappeared out a window … only to reappear a moment later. "Oh, I forgot to tell you about the new gentleman who arrived in Hightower and who is staying with the Flaxseeds in Kendra's old room. Such a mysterious yet handsome man, and I think he's noble. I just thought you might want to know about him."

Then she was gone again, without even sharing the gentleman's name. Ah, well. Emmazel could still work with the information she had.

"Do you really think that marriage is the best way for a woman to improve her station?" asked Heather, shifting her weight from one foot to the other – a nervous habit of hers that she really needed to break.

"I said nothing of *best*," said Emmazel. "Merely that it's the most *interesting*."

"Oh." Heather thought about that for a long moment. "What about you? I've heard that your companions always marry, but you never do."

"Ah," said Emmazel, drawing the word out. "But what higher position would I find? I live in a *tower.*" She laughed at her own joke. "In all honesty, it would require the truest love to tempt me away, for I already have all that I want here."

"Do you?" Heather tilted her head to the side. "Even trapped like you are?"

"I'm not trapped," Emmazel answered. "I can't leave the tower, no, but it's for my safety. It's not safe for someone like me in the world outside. And since I have everything I could want here, what reason could I have to leave? There's *no one* higher than me – I live in a tower!"

She gave a self-satisfied grin at her humor.

"Oh," said Heather, nodding thoughtfully. Emmazel held back a sigh – her wit was lost on her current companion. *Such a shame.* "I'm glad you're happy. Even if your companions keep leaving you."

"My companions only leave when they find another life that will make them happier," Emmazel explained. "It would be selfish of me to keep them here if they're happier somewhere else, no matter what my father might think – oh, but he does have *notions* – but I do hope that if and when you find where *you* are meant to be, you don't tarry here for my sake."

Heather opened and closed her mouth, the line appearing on her brow again as she considered how to protest. "Are you sure?"

"Of course, I'm sure." Emmazel took Heather's hand and squeezed it. "I *want* you to be happy. I *want* you to belong somewhere."

~

Night was quite disgruntled when he arrived home that evening, not even bothering to annoy Emmazel with his typical greeting. He appeared in the window, stalked over to her chair, and then hopped up to perch behind her head.

Instinctively, she reached up to scratch him behind his ears. "What's the matter, little friend?"

The cat didn't answer for several minutes, which meant that

he wasn't sure if her father would like it if he told her the issue bothering him. She felt his tail swish against her ear – he really was upset.

"Does it have anything to do with the new young man staying with the Flaxseeds?" she asked. She doubted this was the case, but making a guess was the best way to make Night talk when he didn't want to talk.

"Where did you hear about him?" asked Night, suspicion edging his question. His tail whipped even harder.

Emmazel rolled her eyes. "Berry was by today, so of *course* she mentioned him. You know how she is."

"Ah, yes, Berry," said Night. "Some days, I wonder why your father allows her to come and fill your ears with gossip the way she does."

"My father insists upon it," Emmazel countered. "I think he's afraid that if he doesn't control the way I gain information, then I'll seek it by means that he doesn't approve. And I *do* need to know what's going on outside, and both you and Father are just so determined to protect me. It's sweet but annoying, you know."

"It is a necessary annoyance, as you well know," said Night.

"Of course it is." Emmazel leaned back, shrugging. "You still haven't told me what's bothering you today. *Does* it have something to do with the visitor?"

"He was asking for you," said Night. "He asked *me* about you. Somehow knew that I could talk even though I hadn't said a word and insisted that I answer."

"Oh," said Emmazel, frowning. "You know, I wasn't quite ready for the next young man to come searching for the maiden in a tower, but I suppose I've gained a bit of notoriety now that Lord Westbrook married one of my girls. Is our guest the prince?"

"He strikes me as a prince, but I don't think he's *our* prince," said Night. "He didn't say his name."

"I'll be sure to find that out when he visits." Emmazel scratched Night under the chin and stood. "What did you tell him about me?"

"As little as I could. And please don't go off and try to match him with Heather. As I told you, I don't trust him, and she doesn't deserve him."

"Look at you, being so open-minded!"

Night jumped down from the chair and disappeared down the stairs. "Open-mindedness has never done me any favors in my life, especially with his sort. I'm going to go see how Heather is coming with supper. I'm hungry."

 "So, how was market today?" asked Emmazel as soon as Heather appeared in the window with a basket of bread and produce on her arm. Visiting the market was, perhaps, one of the most important tasks her companions had, as they sold the potions that Emmazel made, providing them with an income, and then purchasing their supplies for each week.

To Emmazel's surprise, a blush spread across Heather's cheeks. "It was nice," she said simply.

Blushes usually meant an encounter with a handsome young man, and so Emmazel's eyebrow lifted. "Did you meet with anyone?"

She *hoped* it might be the mysterious visitor – oh, but that would make Emmazel's work so much easier! – but knowing Heather, it was likely to be some farmer or worse.

"I met a lot of people," said Heather, drawing back and tucking a stray strand of hair behind her ear. "I was in town, after all, shopping. So I met with the baker, of course. And the butcher. And Farmer Marrin…"

"Farmer Marrin?" Emmazel's eyebrow arched higher. "Wasn't that the family you stayed with before you came here?"

Emmazel hadn't realized that there might be a young man in that family to have turned Heather's head. Oh, but it would be a troublesome affair if it were so!

"Oh, yes, it was!" Heather was bouncing on her toes now, and so Emmazel carefully relieved her of the basket. "Farmer Marrin made sure to ask me how I was doing – he and his sisters were very sorry to have me go, but there really wasn't room for me, and you needed me more."

"I did need you, indeed," said Emmazel. While she typically discouraged Heather's instinct to equate her worth with usefulness, desperate times called for desperate measures. "You know, I don't think you've told me much about the Marrins, for all that you spent a whole year with them."

Heather paused and tugged one of her braids. "Oh, well, I didn't think you wanted to hear about them, you know. They're ever so beneath you, if you know what I mean."

"Just because I live in a tower doesn't mean that I don't care about the people below. Don't forget – I have Berry come as often as possible to share all of the latest gossip. So, really, I find it quite a breach of trust that you should assume my disinterest."

Heather ducked her head, her blush growing. "I'm sorry. I'll remember that, Emmazel."

"Do. And do tell me all about this Farmer Marrin! Is he very old?"

"Oh, no, not at all!" cried Heather, shaking her head. "Well, I mean, he is older than me – but only on the near side of thirty, I assure you."

"And is he … quite common?" Emmazel twisted her hands together, then unfolded them and held them at her sides.

"I think you might think him so, compared to the lords and dukes that visit you," Heather confessed. "But I don't know any lords or dukes, and I think he is a *very* fine farmer."

"Hm," said Emmazel. "Well, that may change for you soon enough – the fact that you've never seen a noble, that is." And hopefully, the regard for Farmer Marrin would topple once Heather was exposed to a proper gentleman.

"Oh!" Heather's blush boomed bright again. "I can't even think of it! To think, me – I know I'm your companion, but I still can't imagine it. Me! Among nobility! Oh – I need to get down to the kitchen and put the food away."

She rushed down the stairs, cheeks blazing. Emmazel chuckled as she watched the girl go. Such innocence!

Oh, but would their mystery prince come soon, regardless of what Night might think of him. What did Night know, really? He was just a talking cat!

And Emmazel was only a girl who had never left her tower.

No, no. No uncertainty – she knew what she was doing, and she did it well. She would see Heather happily settled, or her name wasn't Emmazel. And since her name *was* Emmazel, well! She wasn't in the habit of belying her name.

"Emmazel! Emma, what are you about now, girl?"

Emmazel spun around to see her father standing in the window. She drew herself to her full height and fidgeted with her braid.

"Being a good friend, as you taught me to be," she said, lifting her chin. "Giving a listening ear, paying attention to what interests her. That sort of thing."

Father stared at her narrowly for a long moment and then gave a "harumph," sat down heavily, and closed his eyes. Then it was Emmazel's turn to narrow her eyes as she approached and laid a hand on his shoulder.

"Are you all right, Father?"

He opened his eyes and gave a long sigh. "I'm just getting old, my dear. I've been trying to ignore it, but it's true. I'm an old man, and my years are catching up to me. Soon, I shall blow away with the wind, and who shall be here to protect you?"

Emmazel tensed, not liking to hear her father talk like this. For so long, her life had been a steady rhythm and pattern. So little changed when it was just her, her father, and Night. And her companions, but they were hardly a *fixture* in her life. Not like her father.

If she was to lose her father … she couldn't even think about it. It would break her whole world.

"I'll still have Night," she said, forcing her strongest smile. "You know he won't let anything happen to me."

"He wouldn't, no, but he's just a cat." Father shook his head, opened his eyes, and took Emmazel's hand. "Don't worry about it, my dear. I shall take care of it. Stay in the tower. Take care of your garden. You have no need to think about it."

But the breeze that blew around them was restless.

Emmazel nodded. "Yes, of course, Father."

And she would try to put it out of mind, like a dutiful daughter should – but how could she do it, entirely?

"Leave me be, dear. I'm going to take a nap."

Nodding, Emmazel stood and went up to her garden.

~

Father wouldn't talk about it again, but Emmazel also dared not bring it up. She considered talking to Night … but talking to him about anything so serious would make it real, and she wasn't ready for it to be real.

And, besides, her father had told her to not think about it, and talking to Night *would* be thinking about it.

The next time Berry visited, Emmazel encouraged her to send the guest her way. Improving Heather's life would distract her from the uncertainty of her own future. She still hadn't learned the young man's name, but perhaps it was best that way. After all, what was more romantic than an air of mystery?

The young man was good enough to arrive in a timely fashion, when both Emmazel and Heather were in the sitting room, reading.

"Emmazel! Emmazel! Let down your hair!"

Emmazel stiffened at the unfamiliar voice, and it took every ounce of her self-composure to *not* roll her eyes. Night must have told him how to gain entry to the tower, and he *did* love to annoy her.

She rushed to the window and peered out. A man stood below, but, of course, she couldn't see him well due to the height of the tower.

"Good day, sir!" she shouted down to him. "I'm afraid that you've been misinformed about the strength of my hair, but I will let you in, even so."

She directed the vines to unwind so he could climb them. He took a step back, and she wondered if he was going to run, as some did at this stage, but then he climbed up the vines faster than any young man previous.

Emmazel turned away and sat down again before he appeared in the window and climbed into the room.

He was *quite* a handsome man, she noted with approval. Tall and lean, his messy brown hair hanging in his eyes. She wasn't exactly of his age, but he seemed to be old enough to court Heather, but not too old. His bearing was noble, and he didn't have the dirtiness of a commoner.

She gave Heather a surreptitious glance and gave another nod of approval to see a blush reddening her cheeks. Good. Soon, all thoughts of Farmer Marrins would be wiped from the girl's silly mind.

"Well," he said as he finished his own examination of the room and two ladies within, though he didn't leave the window, and sat against the sill instead, arms folded over his chest. "I'm not sure what I expected to find here, but this is a charming scene indeed." He leaned against the window, folded his arms over his chest, and nodded towards Emmazel. "I take it you're the famed Emmazel I've heard so much about."

"I am," she answered, then inclined her head towards Heather. "And this is my dear companion, Heather."

He turned to regard Heather, tilting his head to the side thoughtfully. "I'm honored to make your acquaintances."

"Oh, of course," said Emmazel. "But can you call it an acquaintance if we don't know *your* name? You have us at a disadvantage – and it's not fair at all."

The man opened his mouth, but then she cut him off again.

"Ah, but if you value your anonymity so much, you don't have to say all of it. Give us a letter to call you by!"

He raised his eyebrows. "A letter, eh? I suppose you mean the first letter of my name. E, then. You may call me E, if that's what you'd like."

"A delightful letter," said Emmazel, as she was quite partial to the letter herself. "Well, Sir E, what brings you our humble village and my tower specifically?"

"Sir E" laughed. "I heard rumors, and I followed them, that's all. A fair maiden trapped in a tower, whose companions had married throughout the nobility in this country, why! It was a mystery no man could refuse."

"Of course not," said Emmazel. She fidgeted with her braid. "So, now that you are here to solve the mystery, go ahead with your questions – what all do you want to know?"

"Have you always lived in this tower, Emmazel?" Sir E asked. "You've clearly lived here a while to have had the village name itself for you. Hightower."

Emmazel sat up straight – that was a question her visitors rarely asked – especially not so soon. Usually, they started with the *why*. Why was she in this tower? Everyone who heard about her *knew* that she'd been there for years.

"As long as I can remember," she answered. "I dream of a forest sometimes, but this tower is the only home I've truly known."

"I see." Sir E gave a slow nod. "And why do you stay here? The rumors say that it's your father who keeps you. Yet, you should be old enough to choose such things for yourself."

"And I choose to stay in the tower," Emmazel answered. "It's not safe out there for one of my kind."

"Ah, yes, one of your kind." Sir E glanced towards the vines in the window. "You're not the first Sensitive that I've met. There are other places you could live without fear, but I suspect you're comfortable in this tower."

Emmazel's heart missed a beat at the thought of living *somewhere else,* but she kept her tone light. "I am quite comfortable here, I assure you."

He nodded. "And this forest you dream of, it doesn't call you?"

This time, Emmazel's smile *did* falter. "It used to," she confessed. "But not in years."

"Interesting." Sir E gave another nod. "Well, I don't think I should like to still be here when your father returns, and so I should be on my way. A fascinating meeting, though. You're an interesting woman, Emmazel, and your companion is quite charming."

He nodded to Heather and then disappeared out the window. As soon as he was gone, Emmazel practically jumped out of her chair, clapping her hands together. "Oh, what did you think of *that*, Heather. A fine man, to be certain – and with *such* taste! He called you charming! Did you notice?"

Heather's cheeks were bright red again, very good – oh, but the dear girl was so obvious! "I did. But all he did was ask about you, and he said you were *interesting*. I just sat here, staring stupidly!"

*Staring stupidly* was good. It meant that he'd caught her interest and that she cared what he thought of her. Emmazel gave a careless wave.

"Oh, any man finds the *maiden of the tower* interesting!" she explained. "I'm a mystery, but he knows that I'm unattainable. You! *You* he called charming. And when a man calls a girl charming, it means that his heart is half gone already."

One love potion would do the trick nicely. Emmazel would prepare the ingredients tonight. She'd not gotten a promise of return from Sir E, that was true, but she doubted he could stay away. He was a man, and they were two maidens in a tower. It was only a matter of time.

"You really think so?"

"My dear Heather, this is what I *do!*"

**5** But, of course, Night would never be so gracious as to let Emmazel have her success uncriticized. As she gathered the ingredients for the love potion, he slunk into her garden room and twisted around her ankles.

"I heard you had a guest today."

Emmazel plucked off some poppy petals and laid them in her basket. "Yes, I did. Sir E was quite charming. He made *such* an impression on dear Heather.

"*Did* he now?" The words were hissed out so low, Emmazel knew they were for himself, not her. "Sir *E*? Did you not even bother to get his *name* this time? Emmazel, do you not take this seriously at all, or has your obsession with this matchmaking business overcome your common sense?"

Emmazel's lips pursed as she added spearmint to the basket. "Rest assured that I *do* plan to learn his name eventually. There's a process to this sort of thing that a cat like you just wouldn't understand. Today was spent answering *his* questions. There will be time enough to sate my own curiosity in the days to come."

"Oh, *is* he returning?"

"They always do." Emmazel bent down to scratch Night behind his ears. "And if he doesn't, another will come, even more deserving of our Heather."

"Must you be so eager to get rid of her? Emmazel, can't you

savor a friendship?"

"It's hardly my fault that a likely candidate appeared so quickly," she answered. "And I have as yet to banish *you* from my tower, dear Night, and I don't see why I need to *keep* anyone else." Emmazel turned now to the hyssop tree to collect some leaves.

"You aren't always going to have your father."

She froze for a heartbeat, panic prickling across her skin before she composed herself and eased a smile into place. "Must you speak of such a dreadful future? Next, you'll tell me that you plan to abandon me and become a barn cat instead."

"Never so long as I live," Night promised. "I've promised your father that I would stick by you no matter what, and I'm a cat of my word. But I cannot visit the market and fetch supplies. You will need a human companion for that, so stop selling them off."

Emmazel took a measured breath and added a turnip to her basket. "I will not hold anyone here against their will if they'll be happier elsewhere. This tower is my prison and no one else's."

Night pulled away and didn't answer for a long minute.

"This tower is to keep you safe. I know it feels like a prison, but—"

"Sir E says that there are others like me. Who … who don't live in towers." Emmazel choked down a sob before Night could hear it. Lavender. She needed lavender for the potion next.

"And he would know, wouldn't he?" Night didn't even try to disguise the bitter edge of his voice. "Emmazel, there are others like you, yes, but none of them *are* you. *You* are not safe if you leave this tower. Please, I know it isn't fair that you must stay here, but you must. I do not trust your Sir E. I don't think that he is here to be your friend. Just … just be careful and remember that not every charming smile is yours to sell. Keep Heather by you, for *she* can be the loyal friend you need."

Night didn't even let her retort, for he disappeared down the stairs before she could form her answer. Annoying cat.

Emmazel turned back to her plants as she tried to school her thoughts back into place. She wasn't bitter about her life in the tower, and she never had been.

But, between Sir E's questions, her father's health, and Night's confession, a door had been jarred open, revealing motives and desires that she'd never let herself ponder.

Rose petals were the last ingredient, and then she laid the basket of herbs on her worktable. Her confusion could be ground to dust with her mortar and pestle, couldn't it?

Perhaps she would need a permanent companion soon, but that day wasn't *here*. Heather had spent her life at the mercy of what others needed from her. She deserved the luxurious life of a noble lady.

Emmazel would find a new companion. Perhaps one of her former companions could send a servant. Or several servants, so she could have a rotation, and none would have to stay trapped in the tower with her. Well, then she might face the issue of rumors and gossip, but didn't she already have that by marrying her companions off to lords? Her father hated it, but he worried *far* too much.

Her father was growing old.

She shook that thought away. Her father didn't want her worrying, so she wouldn't.

What was she going to do without him?

~

The love potion was warm and reassuring in her pocket as Emmazel went about her tasks the next day. She didn't know when Sir E would return, but she would be ready when he did.

After brushing and rebraiding her hair, Emmazel clucked her tongue as she examined Heather. "We should do your hair, too. I have some ribbons that would look delightfully quaint with your freckles. You should wear them!"

Heather, naturally, drew back, her eyes widening in adorable horror. "Your ribbons? Oh, no, I can't, I—"

"I have more ribbons than I need, and who will see me in them?" Emmazel shook her head. "No, they're much better off in your hair – you'll be doing me a favor, really."

"Really?" Heather blinked and reached to fidget with one of her braids. "Are you sure?"

"Of course!" Emmazel picked the brush back up and motioned for Heather to sit down with her back to her. "My father has spoiled me with more gifts than I know what to do with. Thinks that it can make up for my loss of freedom, I suspect, though he'll never say so. Ah, but he's a good father, for all his flaws."

Heather winced.

"Oh, did I pull your hair – I do need to be more careful!" Emmazel chided herself for the careless words. Heather was *so* delicate! "And I'm sure *your* father would have been amazing, had he been in your life."

"Maybe," said Heather. "But he wasn't."

Emmazel chewed her lip as she wove the ribbons into Heather's braids. What had happened to her calm collection? Heather wasn't the first scared young girl who she had helped find confidence and security.

Or maybe this was all just part of the process. Yes, that was it. She had to make Heather face her insecurities so she could move past them.

"You are a beautiful, intelligent young woman. It is his loss that he wasn't there to watch you grow up."

"I suppose."

"Emmazel! Do you mind if I visit you again today?

Emmazel had just tied off the second braid, and she sprang to her feet in delight at Sir E's voice.

"Oh, he came back! I *told* you that you were more than he could resist." She squeezed Heather's shoulder and then rushed to the window so she could hang out. Yes, there was Sir E below them. Oh, but he was a good man!

"One moment!" she shouted down to him before asking the vines to give him entry. He was in the room within moments.

"Ah, but that is a climb!" he declared as he leaned in the window again. "You are not the most welcoming host, Miss

Emmazel. Or, perhaps, your father isn't."

"Alas, he's determined to keep me as safe as possible," Emmazel answered. "Which makes me all the more grateful to have guests. Sir E – oh, but silly me! I declared you a knight, but I don't know if that's true! You seem to be noble, but I have so little experience with the outside world that I can't be certain." She shook her head. "Heather, what do you think? Is our guest a knight? A prince, perhaps?"

Heather gasped, her cheeks flushing bright red again. "I think – I think – I don't know…"

"I am a prince." Sir E rescued her. "Not of this country – I'm sure even you know that Howsill's prince is Christian. You probably haven't heard of my country, however, for I had never heard of this one until a few years ago. So, I shall respect the anonymity that you wanted from me."

"Of course." Emmazel nodded, satisfied. Sir E was a very good man, indeed, and Heather was a very lucky young lady. "But it is good to have that cleared up – though, would you prefer that we call you *Prince* E? *Sir* E just has *such* a delightful ring to it…"

Sir E laughed. "You may address me how you prefer. I am not particular."

"Excellent, Sir E it is," Emmazel decided. "So, are you here to ask more questions, or did you only come to admire Heather's new ribbons. They look *so* lovely in her hair, don't they?"

Sir E's eyebrow lifted as he examined Heather's hair. "They are indeed, and they look even lovelier in her hair."

And his compliment was loveliest of all.

"But I do have questions, of course," he continued, turning again to Emmazel. "A girl in a tower is just too intriguing a mystery for me to stay away from."

"Naturally." Emmazel laughed, then stood. "Oh, but you must be thirsty after your climb into the tower. I should go get you something to drink. Heather, you don't mind keeping our guest entertained for a minute on your own? No? I shall be back as quickly as I can, then."

Emmazel rushed downstairs before either could protest. Sir E was perfect, and a love potion had to be applied as soon as possible. It could be reversed if things went wrong, but luring a gentleman back if he lost interest was a far more impossible challenge.

She slipped the love potion out of her pocket as she reached the kitchen and set it on the counter. Now, what would Sir E prefer to drink? Water didn't conceal the taste of the potion, but people could respond so negatively to either tea or wine.

Well, some wine would be quicker to prepare. She carefully filled half a glass with water, added the potion, and then topped it off with their best wine. Not enough to inebriate him, but the alcohol would help the potion work faster.

When she returned upstairs, Heather was explaining her foundling history, and Sir E was listening attentively. Emmazel slipped the glass into his hand, and he took it and drank, hardly sparing a glance her way to say thank you.

Emmazel smiled as she sat back down with some sewing. She *was* good at what she did. Why had she ever doubted herself?

Sir E came nearly daily after that, always with a story or two to entertain them and always ready to compliment Heather in some form or fashion. Night kept away during his visits and would then make sure to snark and complain after the man left. No one mentioned her father's age or him *dying*, and so all was happy once more.

Emmazel could breathe easy again. Her life was back in order. Yes, her father was still old, but that wasn't her problem to worry about. It *wasn't.*

"Emmazel! Emmazel! Let me back up into the tower! I have the strangest news to share with you, and I don't know what to do about it!"

She rushed to the window at Heather's cry, sending down the vines for her to enter. "Oh, yes, tell me all!" she encouraged.

"Farmer Marrin has proposed to me!" The girl cried, her face flushed as she entered through the window. "They've missed having me, even if they didn't have room. But if I marry him, that won't be a problem. I won't need to share a bed with Zara and Elisa; I'll share with—" She cut herself off, flushing an even brighter shade of red. Emmazel hadn't thought that possible.

The amount of blood rushing to Heather's face was hardly the most alarming aspect of the situation. Emmazel schooled her face and forced a cheerful smile.

"Oh? Really? What did you say? Will I need to help you pack? So soon?"

Heather drew back, recollecting her thoughts as she shook her head. "Oh, I didn't tell him anything. It was so sudden that I didn't know what to think, so I said I would need time to consider, and now I'm back here. Emmazel, what do you think? What should I do?"

Emmazel took a deep breath. Thank Austere for Heather's timidity! All was not lost. "I think you should consider such an important decision very carefully. I can't make it for you, but I'm certainly here to be a listening ear. My father may hate change, but you know that all I want is for my companions to be happy and settled. But so soon! Why, you're hardly settled here!"

"Oh, Emmazel, you really wouldn't mind?" Heather wrung her hands as she sat down, looking more confused than ever. "I told Farmer Marrin that you needed me and that I didn't know if I could leave you."

"Oh, I do need you." Emmazel gave a weak smile as she sat down. "But if this is what will make you happy, if this is what you want – oh, but you *must* be certain, Heather. Marriage is *such* an important decision, and if you are at all uncertain, you should listen to your heart. Is this what you want, Heather?"

Heather rocked back and forth, then laid her head in her hands. "I – I don't know. That's why I'm asking you!"

Emmazel nodded as she felt in control of the situation again. "Your uncertainty makes me wary. Do you care for him?"

"I don't know. I didn't think he saw *me* this way. He's a good man, a good, hardworking farmer who loves his family deeply. I don't know how anyone could know him and not admire him."

"I see." Emmazel was not as in control as she had hoped.

"But why would he want to marry me? Me! Of all the girls in Hightower – you know he could have any he wants, so why would he choose me?"

"I *don't* know that he could have any girl he wants," said Emmazel. "I do, however, know that *you* are a very beautiful and good-natured girl, eager to please, and of *course* any and every young man with a pair of eyes and common sense would fall in love with you at once. My dear Heather, do *not* underestimate your own charm! It would be a grave error for you to hand over your heart to the first young man to *voice* such an attraction purely as a reward for *being* the first."

"A grave error?" Heather echoed. "Do you really think—"

"I'm only counseling you, as you asked." Emmazel held up an empty hand of peace. "If this farmer is truly what you want, then that is one thing, but don't accept him *just* because you don't think someone better will come along. Because if you don't think that Farmer Marrin is the best man ever, then a better *will* come along."

Heather took a deep breath and chewed her lip. "Well, I don't know if I think he's the *best* ever. He's certainly a *good* man, but is he the best? I wouldn't know."

"Think of Sir E," Emmazel pushed forward. "If you were to put them side-by-side, how do they compare?"

"Sir E?" Heather's voice rose in a panicked pitch as she flushed red again. "Do you really think he…"

"Oh, he's quite taken with you, I'm sure," said Emmazel. "Have you not wondered that he keeps coming to visit?"

Heather shook her head in distress. "He comes to visit you, I'm sure!"

"Perhaps at first, but he spends most of his visits talking to you! He's quite enamored, I promise. Don't you remember how he complimented your hair ribbons?"

"Yes, of course, but—"

"Now, I really can't counsel you one way or another, but I do think that your refusal should be firm but kind," Emmazel continued. "He's laid his heart before you, and you must respect that. But you must not give him false hope if he has none. Give him back all of the strings of his heart so he can focus his intentions on one of those other deserving girls."

"You think I should refuse him?" Heather's voice rose

again.

"I don't *think* anything," Emmazel insisted. "My opinions mean nothing, I promise. But you are too uncertain to give him a yes. Perhaps if he was a lord or a prince and could offer you a life of ease, but he's a farmer."

"There's nothing wrong with farmers!" Heather cried.

"Oh, of course," Emmazel agreed. "Farmers are good men, the best of men, but you can't deny that life as a farmer's wife is difficult. If you're sure you love him, that's well and good, for they say that a crust of bread in a house of love is sweeter than a feast in a house of strife. But *I* say that if one is going to settle, then it's best to settle for the feast."

Heather took a deep breath and nodded. "And you think that I am settling?"

"Are you?"

"I—" Heather pressed both of her fists to her temples. "I don't know. Oh, Emmazel, this is all so sudden, and whatever I choose will change everything. I wish that he had never asked me!"

"If you wish that he hadn't asked, then I would consider that an emphatic *no*," said Emmazel.

Heather sat straight, blinking as her hands fell to her lap. "Oh. I see. I – oh, Emmazel, what do I tell him? He'll be so disappointed. I fear that my tongue shall get all twisted, and I'll accept him out of pity if I should look at him again."

"And that would never do," Emmazel agreed. "But have no fear; I shall help you as I can. I would recommend a letter, but those are so impersonal, and we don't even know if he can read!"

"Oh, he can!" Heather interjected, agitated again. "He's very well educated and has a whole collection of farmer's manuals he's quite proud of."

"Farmer's manuals. How … quaint." Emmazel blinked as she processed this new information. "Well, a rejection letter is still too impersonal. Come now, let's practice exactly what to say until there's no chance for you to say anything else."

~

It was exhausting. Heather was such a bundle of nerves, stumbling over even the most simple of scripts, and this was only the rehearsal! They wound up writing a letter, after all, just in case.

"Now, I know you want to rush back and give him your answer immediately, but wait a while – you must appear that you *thought* it over," Emmazel had further counseled. "Keep that letter in your pocket until your next visit to the market, and put the whole affair out of mind until then. Worrying won't make it come faster or slower, and there are so many more things more pleasant to think about – such as Sir E's next visit!"

Then she dismissed Heather to fix dinner and went upstairs to tend her garden and straighten her own nerves. Today had been so nearly a disaster, and it could still be so if Heather lost her nerve and accepted this farmer's suit.

But that *would* not happen. Could not. Emmazel would make sure of it – as best she could.

"Emmazel, Emmazel, how easily your plots and plans can come to naught."

This was, of course, Night's obnoxious taunt and *not* Emmazel's own inner critique. She was *not* so descended into uncertainty that she was chiding herself in *his* voice.

She spun around and crossed her arms over her chest. "What do you know? What makes you assume that the world is not, in fact, falling directly into place according to my plans?"

Night stalked past her, hopped up on her desk, and wrapped his tail around himself, looking *quite* smug and self-satisfied. "I have it on the best authority that Heather is about to be *very* well settled. The young farmer she stayed with last is very taken with her, and *I* predict that the match shall be made within the week, if it has not already."

Emmazel scoffed loudly – she couldn't help herself. "Oh, you silly cat! Whatever made you fix on such a match? I'm sure even you realize that Heather is meant for much more than the life of a farmer's wife."

"And what is wrong with being a farmer's wife?" asked Night. "It is a noble profession, and he is a good man. He will take care of her."

"He will work her to death! What do you know about marriage? You're a cat!"

"And you live in a tower. I know far more about marriage than you." Night licked his paw. "I know you have your heart set on a royal wedding for Heather, but it is *not* to be."

"Just because he has fixed his affections on her doesn't mean that the match is sure," said Emmazel. "*I* have it on good authority that she fled the proposal in alarm and her rejection has been penned."

Night looked up from his paw, his ears laid back. "Penned by your own hand, I'm sure."

"I may have helped her perfect the wording, but she wrote every line herself." Emmazel twisted away and grabbed her tray of seedlings to plant. "Oh, Night, you should have seen her relief as she realized that she didn't have to marry him just because he asked and she admired him."

"She admired him, and you still broke them up. Emmazel, you—"

"I did nothing of the sort!" Emmazel stabbed the soil with her shovel. "I counseled her to help her know her own mind, but you should have seen her distress! No, Night, she is *not* best off married to this farmer, and you cannot convince me otherwise."

"If she's confused, it's only because you've twisted her mind and convinced her that she deserves more than is her due."

Emmazel sent him a glare over her shoulder. "I thought you wanted her to never marry so she can take care of me for the rest of her life. How is she supposed to do that if she must also care for this farmer?"

"Far easier than she could if she was shipped off to another country," Night countered. "And you're determined that she not spend the rest of her life trapped in the tower with you. If she marries and settles nearby, she can still bring you supplies and gossip, but still her live her own life."

Emmazel blinked as she realized that Night's logic *did* make sense. Sense that she could even appreciate. Still…

"I *refuse* to believe that a farmer is the best she can do. She's a nobleman's daughter. I'm sure of it."

"But you have no way to know that for certain," Night countered. "Stop trying to fit her into your idea of who you think she should be. You *will* be disappointed."

"What do *you* know about Heather's hopes and dreams?" Emmazel countered. "You've never so much as spoken to her."

That jab must have struck, for Night didn't answer for the longest time. When he finally did, it was a subdued, "We shouldn't quarrel, Emmazel. We both want what is best for Heather."

Emmazel twisted around to answer, but he was already slipping back downstairs.

Sir E had left not minutes before another voice summoned Emmazel back to the window. There stood the last person she had expected to return – her previous companion, Anna. Quickly, Emmazel ordered the vines to give her friend entry.

Anna was an older woman in her mid-thirties, a decided old maid until Emmazel had worked her magic. Father had thought himself quite clever in recruiting her, but he had underestimated Emmazel, as usual.

"Ah, Emmazel, dear child – you're looking quite as well as ever!" Anna beamed as she climbed through the window and sized Emmazel up and down. "Oh, but I haven't missed climbing in and out of this window. Would it really have been the end of the world for your father to have installed a proper door in this tower?"

Emmazel shrugged and shook her head at Anna's typical complaint. "He's a Zephyr, you know. Doesn't need a door himself when he dissipate into the wind itself, so here we are."

Besides, the lack of a door made it that much easier to keep one's daughter inside.

No, no, banish that thought. It didn't do her any good.

"True enough," said Anna, throwing herself into a chair. "And I didn't come to complain about your window, horrid thing it might be. Oh, no. If that were the case, I would have stayed well away. But you needed company, my dear friend, that's the long and short of it, and since I still live close enough to make a day of it, I'll certainly do just that."

"Thank you," Emmazel said earnestly as she sat down.

Anna waved off the gratitude. "Don't worry about it, dear child! And, yes, yes, you say that you're nearly as old as I am, or older, but I'll always think of you as the daughter I never had. I'll do anything I can for you."

Emmazel's smile turned into a wry grin. "You might have a daughter of your own, soon enough."

"True, but that can't keep me from loving you as my own, just as much!" Anna reached over and patted Emmazel's hand. "I'm getting older, so I don't know how much time I have!"

Something warmed within Emmazel. She'd never had a mother of her own, nor had she ever thought of Anna as one, and yet…

Her father was growing old.

"Now, tell me how you've been, my dear friend," Anna continued when Emmazel was silent. "Who's your companion now – for your father would never let you stay alone for long."

"No." Emmazel's laugh came out harsher than she would have liked. "He doesn't. Her name is Heather, and she is the *most* timid thing there is. A foundling raised by a blacksmith who never appreciated her. The poor girl."

"Oh! Heather!" Anna nodded knowingly. "Your father did mention that she would likely be my successor. She's a good girl, and I can't think of anyone who might deserve this more."

"I quite agree!" said Emmazel, brightening. "Oh, but I already have a young man coming to visit her! A prince! Not our prince, a foreign prince. We call him Sir E, and he is the *most* charming fellow."

"Oh? I heard we had a visiting prince," said Anna. "A very mysterious fellow and no one knows much about him. Has he really made his way here? Emmazel! Your reputation has grown, hasn't it?"

"Yes," Emmazel agreed, though she suddenly wondered if this *was* a good idea. With someone agreeing with her, it suddenly lowered her defenses and let her see everything horridly wrong with it. After all, she was supposed to be secret and safe in her tower, and now she wasn't.

But there were others like her who lived outside, Sir E said. While Night insisted that *she* was still not safe if she left the tower.

"I'm determined to do all I can for her," she declared, gathering her thoughts back together. "She's such a dear, you know."

"I always thought as much," said Anna. "I always wanted to help her, but an old maid doesn't have many resources. I always thought we might be able to work together against the world, she and I, if she were ever abandoned, but your father invited me to live here before the blacksmith's family tired of her."

Emmazel nodded. "It would have been a hard life."

"Yes, but it would have been easier together, and thank Austere it never came to it! Really, you and your father are more generous than I think either of you realizes."

"My father just wants to keep me safe, you know, and if the situation can benefit girls without other options, then that just makes it better," Emmazel answered. "I, though … I want to do what I can. I live in a tower; people take care of me. What am I supposed to do?"

"You provide all sorts of herbs and potions for Hightower," Anna reminded her. "You are not useless, I tell you! Though, I do confess that rumors call you the witch of the tower. No one really knows much about you, after all."

"What?" Emmazel sat up straighter.

Anna just waved her off again. "Oh, yes. It keeps you safe. They fear you, but they also depend on what you supply them. Don't worry, my dear, *dear* child. You are quite secure in your tower, and you are a burden to no one."

Emmazel forced her smile back into place, even as she shifted uncomfortably. She didn't like how Anna could see through her – and yet it felt so nice to be *seen*. "You know, I could probably make you a potion or two, if you'd like them. To help improve your chances of conceiving. You're not a young woman, after all, and I'm told it gets harder with age."

It was Anna's turn to give a harsh laugh as she leaned back. "It's not why I came to see you, but I'd be lying if I said that the offer doesn't mean the world to me. I do want children of my own and to give my husband an heir. Emmazel, you've done far too much for me already, but I know you. I'll accept the gift."

Emmazel nodded as she stood and led the way up the stairs, her mind too full of spinning thoughts to answer.

"It *is* a shame to have you trapped in this tower," Anna continued. "You're so bright and loving, and I just know there's the right young man for you out there."

"Are you trying to encourage me to leave this tower?" Emmazel reached for the ingredients for the potion she knew well, for it sold well at market. "My father wouldn't be happy if he heard you, you know!" She forced a laugh.

"Perhaps not, but you are a grown woman, and you deserve to be treated as one, not a child – especially if you're nearly as old as I am, as you say." Anna shook her head. "He means well. I know that. And I know that you and he are both stranger than I can ever understand. But you deserve some freedom, and you deserve to be loved as a woman. It will have to be a special young man, though!"

"Of course, it would be," Emmazel answered. "Why would I give up all of this for anything less than the best?" She motioned weakly about the room.

"The best you say? Naturally! And who's better than our Prince Christian himself? I've met him now – and such a charming young man he is! I can't think of a single young man more deserving."

"But for him to come here and visit me?" asked Emmazel. "Is that likely? He's a prince and surely has duties to attend to!"

"And surely so does every other young man who has come to seek you out in this tower." Anna shook her head. "Prince Christian is intrigued by you, as much as any young man ever has been, and I think you would be wise to keep him for yourself. You would be an excellent queen, after all."

Emmazel pressed her lips into a line of concentration as she finished the potion and handed it to Anna. "You know the instructions for this, for you've sold it for me plenty of times. May it serve you well. I – I can't ever leave my tower, as you well know. I can't leave my father."

Thankfully, Anna didn't push the issue, and Emmazel was soon left alone again.

~

The next morning was one of Berry's visits, right on schedule, and Emmazel was still flustered by Anna's visit. But, still, in the fairy flew, bursting to share Kendra Flaxseed's latest letter.

So, Emmazel steeled her nerves as best she could and invited the fairy upstairs. Berry followed her, already chattering away as though she noticed nothing else about the world except her own voice and her darling Kendra.

"She thinks she might be returning home soon!" the fairy suddenly declared, flying around Emmazel's head.

Emmazel blinked, freezing as she reached for one of her rose trees. "Will she now?"

"Perhaps, perhaps, she doesn't know for sure." Berry landed on a leaf. "I don't know what Lady Camilla will do without her; the two are such dear friends. But Kendra says she may be leaving her friend, so I can't wait to see the dear girl again. She's been gone four years, you know. Ages! I know it doesn't seem so long for you, but it's truly far too long to be away from one's home. Why, my family has served the Flaxseeds for as far back as any can remember, and none of us would even think to leave. Oh, she must be pure confusion, being away so long, yet not wanting to leave her post!"

"I suppose that must be why she's going to come home, then. To sort through this confusion."

Emmazel didn't *really* think that this was the case. She hadn't a clue why Kendra might be abandoning her work as a lady-in-waiting, but neither did she care. However, she was talking to a *fairy*.

"Perhaps. If she's coming home. If she can!" Berry was

zooming about the room again. "Oh, oh, can you think of it! The dear girl, home again! I can't believe it. Can you?"

Emmazel bit the inside of her cheek and shook her head. "No, I really can't say that I can."

"Perhaps you can't, for you've never met her – just heard all of her letters." Berry nodded sagely, as though she knew what she was talking about. It was bold to assume that a fairy knew what she was talking about. "You know the importance of staying in your home, in the place where you belong. But, when Kendra returns, I'll be sure to bring her here and let her tell you all of her journeys and adventure. Why, I'm sure it will be even more exciting to hear her tell it all herself!"

Emmazel blinked, but Berry was already disappearing down the stairs again. Fairies! Emmazel really didn't know why she let that one keep coming, taunting her with news of the outside world——

Except she desperately wanted news of the outside world. Why couldn't she be content, the way she had once been?

"Emmazel, are you up here?"

She drew in a breath and pasted on a smile as Heather appeared in the doorway. "Yes, I'm here. Of course. My garden must be tended, after all. Even up here, weeds find a way."

Heather nodded, distantly fingering some basil. "It's so strange, this room. How silent it is. Outside, the plants sing, but here, I feel like I should hear something, but I can't. There's something heavy and solid in the way."

Emmazel stiffened, her pasted smile falling into a frown. "You can hear plants?"

"Yes. Outside, but not here. Can you hear them here?"

"Always, and I can speak to them. How else do you think that I direct them to grow so strong and tall?"

Heather frowned harder, now squeezing the leaf of basil – Emmazel could hear it protest in pain. "I suspected as much. No one else can hear the plants; they always thought I was a bit touched in the head. I didn't say anything since coming here, just in case … but I wondered."

"And you can't hear them in here?"

Emmazel's head was spinning. There were other girls like her, Sir E said. But none that were *her*, Night said. Was Heather one of those girls? Was that why her father had brought her now, and why Night was so determined that she stay?

"No, I can't. As I already told you."

Why? *Why?* Was it the tower? Father and Night both claimed that Emmazel was only safe within this tower. Perhaps it wasn't an outside threat at all, but to keep her safe from *herself*.

"Perhaps…" The word pulled itself out of Emmazel and hung in the air. "Perhaps I should teach you. You aren't confined to the tower, so you can practice outside. If you can hear the plants, you may well be able to talk to them."

"Maybe," Heather agreed. "I think I can, but I never realized it possible."

8 Emmazel didn't teach Heather about speaking to plants. They didn't even talk about it again as the days went past. Emmazel suspected that Heather practiced on her own, outside, but the unspoken fear hung between them.

Why was Emmazel in a tower that dampened such power, and why wasn't it enough to suppress own abilities? Unless it did and she was supposed to be far stronger than she was. Why couldn't she return to the neat, orderly life she'd understood?

Except nothing had changed. Emmazel was just realizing how constrained her life had been and how many questions she should have been asking years ago. Questions that likely had answers she didn't want to face.

"Emmazel, Emmazel, let down your hair!"

Her eyes widened at Sir E's cry, and she rushed to the window, grateful for a distraction. It wasn't until Sir E was in the window when she realized the problem with his visit today.

"I'm afraid Heather isn't here right now," she said, shaking her head. "I'm so sorry! It's market day, so I sent her to sell my potions and to purchase supplies."

A frown creased Sir E's brow for a brief moment, and then he nodded as he leaned against the windowsill. "She mentioned that the market is part of her duties as your companion, and it's one of her favorite duties as well."

"I imagine it is." Emmazel fidgeted as she sat down in her chair. "After all, it's when she gets to leave the tower and mingle with people. I hate keeping her in the tower with me. She deserves freedom."

"No one deserves to be kept in a tower," said Sir E.

"Perhaps not, but some of us are safer in one." Emmazel sighed.

Sir E stared at her for a long, painful moment, neither agreeing nor disagreeing. "It's a sad truth, perhaps."

"It is." Emmazel took a long breath to organize her nerves. "You can probably catch up to Heather if you leave now. She's usually at the market for several hours, so…" Her nerves were not staying as organized as she liked.

"I don't see a reason why," said Sir E. "I only ever seem to talk with her when she's here, so I'd like to take advantage of having you alone to talk to."

"What!" Emmazel sat up straighter.

"Nothing untoward, though I realize how that sounded." Sir E held up a hand of peace. "I've wanted to talk to you alone for a long time, but Heather has always been here with you, and you're very good at slipping away and leaving me speaking only to her. Not that I mind speaking to her, not at all, but you were why I sought out the tower in the first place."

"Right. Of course." Emmazel swallowed. "I'm sorry. I just thought … the two of you … never mind."

If the love potion was weakened, it was best to not push it. She would just need to give him another, the next time he was here *with* Heather. The potion did nothing if the object of affection wasn't there to focus on.

"What would you like to ask me? I'd really thought you had exhausted all of your curiosity. I'm not that interesting, you know."

"Because a maiden in a stone tower, with a braid to her feet is the most mundane thing in existence," said Sir E, his eyebrow rising.

"Well, I've told you all there is to tell about me, at the very least."

Why wouldn't he just leave? Heather was out there, at the market, and if he were to meet her there, why, who knew what might happen. A picnic? A long walk through the woods? He might even take her home to his kingdom here and now!

But, no, he was here, standing before Emmazel, asking questions about *her*.

"Are you actually happy in this tower, and are you sure it's not safe for you to leave?"

Emmazel looked away, unable to hold eye contact with his heart-filled gaze. "I don't know any other life, so of course I'm content. I promise, I'm content. This tower is my home. And, no, I don't think it's safe for me to leave. I believe that more than ever."

"Do you now?"

She looked up to find that he had stepped away from the window. "You know how you said that there are others like me?"

"I did say so, yes." Sir E leaned back against the window again. "Is that worrying you, now? Do you think that there's some particular danger against yourself?"

"I think..." Emmazel caught herself and shook her head. Sir E had no business prying into her secrets like this. "I think Heather might be one of those girls."

"And you would be correct."

Emmazel blinked and sat up straight, having not expected such a boldfaced confirmation of her suspicion. "Really, I—"

"And I suspect that it may be why she was left on the blacksmith's doorstep..." Sir E mused. "And yes, it's probably why you're in this tower. When you were young, it was dangerous for girls of your kind. She's weak enough that merely putting distance between her and danger was enough to protect her, but you ... you, Emmazel, were too strong to hide with mere distance. You needed a tower."

"Oh." Emmazel shifted as she digested his words. There was a threat. A threat to both her and Heather. "So..."

"The Mistress is gone now," Sir E assured her. "But you might well still be best off in this tower. There's a lot outside you know nothing about and that would see you as a threat. And you've never had a chance to learn to manage yourself at full strength." He finished with a shrug. "So I wouldn't blame you if you stay here. And I also apologize for ever suggesting that you should leave."

Emmazel didn't know what to say, so she just ran her braid through her hands. "I don't … I don't know…"

"You!"

She sprang to her feet as her father materialized in the middle of the room.

~

Sir E, in his defense, stayed absolutely calm as Emmazel's father stared him down. He straightened, letting his folded arms fall to his sides as he glanced the old man up and down. A slight frown creased his brow, but he was grinning again as he met her father's gaze. "I was wondering when our paths would cross. You're a terribly hard man to meet with, you know."

"What are you doing in my daughter's tower?"

"Just talking, I assure you." Sir E tilted his head to the side. "My affections lie elsewhere as you undoubtedly know. Or not. I know it didn't go well for you."

Father's frown grew, and then he suddenly slumped back in a chair. "No, it didn't. Young man, you weren't welcome here, but I suppose I couldn't hide forever. She didn't want anything to do with us, but I know her successor wouldn't have her self-satisfied security. What do you want with us? And don't lie."

"Nothing but to know that you and your daughter are well."

"Do we look well?"

"Your daughter certainly does," said Sir E. "But I think you've seen haler days."

Father's laugh was harsh. "I have indeed, and yet now I

relish the freedom. Be off with you, young man. I hope your curiosity is sated. Return with your report and tell the new Mistress that my daughter and I will be no threat to her."

"Can you see so far in the future?"

Emmazel knew nothing of what her father and Sir E said to each other, and she just sat there, running her braid through her hand and twisting it tighter and tighter. She wanted explanations, but she also wanted neither to notice her.

What was going on?

"We will be no threat. Let us live."

"Fear has kept your daughter in the tower for this long, but when you're gone, who will guide her if she ever does leave?" Sir E asked. "I think the Gardener would prefer to foster friendship. After all, she's family."

Father straightened. "Is she?"

"Foxglove's elder daughter." Sir E folded his arms over his chest again. "She's not like her grandmother at all, and I would follow her to the end of the world and back."

"Glowing praise that I shall bear in mind." Father raised a hand, and a gust of wind wrapped around Sir E, lifting him from the floor. "I will need time to think. You should go."

And then he sent Sir E out of the window.

Emmazel's heart was pounding in her ears. What did this mean? What did any of this mean?

She turned her head to find her father staring at her, his eyes narrowed.

"I wish you hadn't been here to overhear that, but I suppose I can't protect you forever. Austere knows I can't protect you forever." Father drew in a deep breath. "You are to never threaten the new Mistress, this Gardener. Do you hear me? Your mother was a wicked woman, and I will not have you follow in her footsteps."

What? Now her father was speaking of her mother? What was world coming to?

"I don't understand," she whispered.

"You don't need to. Stay in this tower. I—"

A coughing fit overtook her father's words. Emmazel sprang up and rushed to his side. It was far easier to deal with her father's failing health than the nagging questions that chased themselves around her head.

Carefully, she helped him downstairs to his room and gave him a tonic to help his lungs. Then she leaned against his bedroom door, took a deep breath, and closed her eyes.

"Everything can stay the same if I stay in this tower," she whispered. "Nothing has to change."

But those words felt so hollow.

Today was so strange, sending her already-scattered pieces into utter chaos.

"Sir E isn't in love with me. He said as much," she added. "His affections lie elsewhere. He has to be in love with Heather, like he's supposed to be. Everything is under control. Everything is fine."

"Are you sure about that?"

Her breath caught as she opened her eyes and found Night on the floor before her, his tale wrapped around himself.

"I – what are you doing here, Night? Spying on me?"

"I'm seeing if you're all right. You seem upset, dear Emmazel, and that seems like such a crime to me."

Emmazel blinked as she stared down at the cat. "Why do you care?"

"I don't know, but if I didn't, I would have left years ago, I promise. You're not the easiest person to get along with. Granted, though, I know that I'm not, either."

"Right." Emmazel took a deep breath and glanced back over her shoulder. "Father never talks about my mother, but today … she says she was wicked. Night…"

"Your mother was the most horrible person I've ever had the misfortune to cross," said Night, licking his paw. "But you aren't her. And I hope you stay like that. So long as you never resemble her, I will stand by you, I promise."

*9* "Heather, how was your day at market?"

Emmazel felt that her question was perhaps *too* desperate as Heather appeared in the window, but what else could anyone expect? She was trapped in a tower, and Heather was her primary connection to the world outside. She always asked for gossip after Heather returned home.

"Oh, it was as good as ever. Except, I saw Elisa, and it was awkward."

Emmazel forced herself to *calmly* raise an eyebrow. "Really? Why is that?"

"Because—" Heather drew the word out and then shook her head. "You know what, it doesn't matter. I rejected her brother, that's all. It's no reason for me to no longer know how to talk to her. It's ridiculous, really. And when I live in another kingdom, I won't care at all, you know."

"I'm sorry," said Emmazel. "That sounds … difficult. But, yes, it should be easier when you live far, far away. Much as … much as I will miss you."

Heather took a sharp breath, set down her basket of supplies, and sat down. "Emmazel, are you all right?"

Emmazel shook herself. "I'm fine, I promise," she said far too quickly.

Heather's frown grew. "Are you sure? Because you've been very upset lately, and you're especially distressed right now. I mean, if you don't want to say anything, that's fine, but … I don't know." She shook her head. "You've done so much for me, and I don't want you to be upset."

"I don't think there's anything you can do about it, besides tell me what's happening outside." Emmazel shrugged and leaned back in her seat. "Which is what you were doing, wasn't it."

Heather brightened. "Of course! Yes! I was. I can do that."

She proceeded to chatter on with all of the enthusiasm she could muster – which was considerable. Yet, Emmazel, try as she might, could barely follow. She didn't know the world outside. She only ever heard about it second-hand. How was she supposed to care about something she had never seen?

How was she supposed to think about a market when Sir E's conversation with her father still circled in her head?

"And that's how I wound up with twice the eggs I normally get," Heather concluded.

Emmazel nodded slowly. "I … I do like eggs. Sir E was here while you were gone." Then she winced as she realized that she'd let that news escape.

Heather sat up straight. "He was? And he's gone already? What happened? I—"

"My father came home and scared him away." Emmazel shook her head. "Don't worry about it. He referred to you as affectionately as ever. Did he not follow after you to the market? I told him you were at the market."

"He didn't, no," said Heather, shaking her head. She bit her lip, looking quite worried.

"No matter," said Emmazel, attempting to wave it off. "My father … upset him a lot, I think. I know I was quite scattered, so I wouldn't blame him if he just went home to lie in bed for a week and think."

"What did your father do?" Heather's eyes went even wider.

Emmazel shrugged. "I don't … I didn't understand it myself. I think Sir E might have ulterior motives for visiting me, but that doesn't mean he's *evil*, you know. Or that his love for you isn't genuine."

"Right, of course," said Heather, slowly nodding.

"He said something about his affections, and I'm sure he meant you. He was assuring my father that he wasn't pursuing me, and my father knows that I help my companions find love." Emmazel stood. "Let's not worry about it. Today has been confusing, but you have twice the number of eggs we normally have, so we need to put them away. Make a cake!"

"Right, of course," Heather repeated, picking the basket back up. "We have fewer apples than normal. The Rimonds' orchard just isn't producing the way it normally is."

"We'll make do," said Emmazel, patting Heather on the shoulder. "And hopefully, you won't have to worry about me for much longer, but shall be a princess in a foreign land. Sir E should propose any day now. It's inevitable. Perhaps the next time he visits!"

Heather bit her lip and nodded. "Hopefully. Are you sure that you'll be all right without me? I think your father was very hopeful that I would stay with you, and if I marry a foreign prince, that will take me far away, and I won't be able to visit at all, the way Anna does. I saw her when she was here, last, you know."

"I shall be *fine*," Emmazel insisted. "You need not worry about me. And whatever villain made your parents abandon you on the blacksmiths' doorstep is dealt with, and it sounds like Sir E knows where you come from, and won't you be so much happier when you're where you belong?"

"Does he? He never said anything about that to me."

"He said…" Emmazel took a deep breath and shrugged. "Perhaps you should ask him about it next time he visits. But he said something about your being abandoned for the same reason that I'm in this tower. For our protection. That might be why my father picked you. Or … something like that. I think he's had his eye on you for a while and has been waiting for the right moment."

"Really?"

"I know he has his plans," said Emmazel, holding up a hand. "But I want you to be happy. I don't want to force you to stand by me. I can't leave this tower. I shouldn't. Even if that villain is gone. My father forbids it."

"I'm so sorry."

"Don't worry about it. I've lived my whole life in a tower – I wouldn't know what to do if I left. I'm much happier here, all around."

"But are you, though? I don't know what I would do without the bright sky overhead and the open fields. The thought of being trapped in here, all of the time! I wouldn't be able to bear it."

"I'm stronger than you," said Emmazel. "I don't … I wouldn't know what to do if I ever left, I'm sure."

~

The days sped by, no one talked about Sir E's meeting with Emmazel's father, and soon she had her thoughts in order again. Emmazel tended her garden, Heather tended the kitchen, Father blew in and out, and Night was generally annoying. Sir E didn't return, which was worrying, but Father had been frightening. Emmazel kept reminding herself that if she'd been on the receiving end of the argument, she would stay away, too.

Heather reported that she met with Sir E twice on her daily walks, which Emmazel now insisted she take, and that was good enough. As long as they were meeting sometime. All was not lost.

"I wish you wouldn't encourage Heather's affection towards that Sir E of yours. He's not for her, as I've said."

Emmazel sighed and sat back on her heels to glare at Night, who sat watching her as she gardened. She didn't know when he'd sneaked into her tower. He was out last time she checked.

"I want her to be happy."

"As though you would be happy if you were encouraged to leave everything you know and care about?" asked Night. "You've lived your whole life in a tower and never want to leave it, and yet you encourage every young maiden you get your hooks into to pull up all their roots and chase after the first young man with a title who shows them a shred of attention. It's not right, Emmazel, and you've gone too far this time."

"And is it too far if Sir E's home country is her place of birth? I think it might be!"

Night opened and shut his mouth, considering, and then he shook his head. "It might have been, but everyone who loves and cares about her is here."

"Such as the blacksmith and his wife who cast her out as soon as she wasn't useful to them?" asked Emmazel. "Or the farmer who just wanted her to work herself to death at his side?"

"Such as us."

"Oh? Father and I would keep her trapped in a tower, and you've never even spoken to her. No, I think if Sir E will give her a home, it will be a much better one than ours." Emmazel turned back to her flowers and poured all of the affection she had into them.

"Emmazel, you can't keep throwing friends away because you think you destroy their lives," Night added. "She will stand by you, willingly, if you would only let her."

"Not her."

"He's going to break her heart."

Emmazel froze, blinking. "What? What makes you ever think a thing like that?"

"Because he doesn't love her the way you think, and you've convinced her to pour all her affection on him. She's never had a true home. She's vulnerable."

"You think he doesn't love her, I—"

"You might have given him a love potion, but you know as well as I do that those don't last, and they aren't real," said Night. "And I've watched them together too many times, especially on their walks just now. I think he only talks to her to get information about you, and I don't like that. He knows too much, and he always has."

Emmazel pressed her lips together as she thought back to her last conversation with Sir E. And the conversation he'd had with her father. "Maybe he does, but that doesn't mean he can't love Heather. They're positively sweet together!"

"I think you see only what you want to see when you look at them. He's polite, and she's bashful. That's not romance."

"It could be! It could be an excellent start to one!" Emmazel shook her head.

"And maybe you've fixed on the first young man to come through your window because that's how you think love works in your tiny, warped world."

"Hateful cat!"

"Ah, and now we resort to name calling because you have no real arguments to that," Night walked past her and lashed her with his tail. "It's no way to win a debate, my dear young friend, not even in your small world."

"I can't help that I can't leave this tower, and you know exactly why I have to stay. Far better than I do, I'm sure."

"Emma—"

"I thought I understood my life, but I don't." Emmazel took a deep breath. "Sir E and Heather, they've both opened up so many questions, and now I think I just want them both gone. As soon as possible. Much as I love Heather and find her a dear friend. I'm not made for friendship."

"I think you are; you just are afraid of your walls," said Night. "And I think that's why I stay, no matter how much you frustrate me."

"Thank you." And Emmazel really did mean it. Night might be frustrating, but he had always been there.

"Stop trying to push Heather away. I think she *can* be the friend you don't allow yourself to have, if you would only allow her." Night batted at Emmazel's hand until she rubbed him behind the ear, absentmindedly. "And if you have questions, you can ask them. I don't promise answers, but I'll tell you what I can."

"Really?" Emmazel frowned.

"What I can," Night repeated.

"All right then." She chewed her lip as she thought. Sir E had already answered a lot of her questions, cracking open more that she didn't quite want to face. And she knew that both Night and her father had their secrets. Night could never speak about his past, after all, could never tell anyone how he came to be a *talking* cat, or else he would lose the ability to talk. What questions could she ask that would have answers she was willing to face? Which would he be able to answer?

"The villain that both Heather and I had to hide from, was she my mother?"

"Yes."

The word was so heavy, but Night said it without hesitation. Or explanation. It made Emmazel's heart sink even lower within her. No wonder her father didn't like to talk about her, if he had to hide his own daughter from the woman he'd married.

"Why haven't you spoken to Heather, even though you seem to care so much about her?"

He did hesitate with this answer, and Emmazel briefly wondered if it might have something to do with his past.

"Because neither of us is ready. Please don't send her away."

# 10

"Emmazel, have the vines ready. Your 'Sir E' will be here shortly to talk to you."

"What?" Emmazel blinked as she stared at her father. "I thought you never wanted to see him again."

"I believe I said I would consider the branch of peace that he offered. I have decided to accept. And it begins with allowing him to explain things to you."

"What sort of things?"

"The things I find too painful to say." Father took a heavy breath and shook his head. "I'm afraid I'm a coward, my dear daughter. This young man will explain things to you, and then you can make decisions about what you will do after I am gone."

"You're not leaving me *now*, though, Father!" Emmazel folded her arms over her chest.

"Austere willing, no." Father gave a tired laugh. "But it will still be best if you learn things now."

"Then—"

"Emmazel! Let down the vines, please, will you?"

It was Sir E, here already. Emmazel glanced at her father. "But—"

"Let him in, dear, or I think he'll do it himself. He's nearly as strong as you, after all."

And so Emmazel woodenly went to the window and ordered the vines to let Sir E into the tower. She couldn't disobey her father, after all. Not when he looked at her like that, his heart nearly breaking in his eyes.

She frowned at him as he came through the window. He didn't linger there today and instead settled into one of her chairs. His grin was gone, and he stared at Emmazel with a determined stare. "The Gardener sent me to find you Emmazalea. To let you know that she would not fight you if you desire peace."

"That sounds … nice of her," said Emmazel, frowning deeper. She'd never heard a longer version of her name, but it sounded almost *right*. Like it should have fit her, but because she never used it, it was now all wrong. "But why would I not desire peace? I don't know her."

"Because she took the throne that rightfully belongs to you."

"*What?*" Emmazel glanced towards her father, wishing that he was the one explaining. He would know what to say and what to avoid, but … he also would say nothing. "Are you saying that my mother, who Night has told me is why I'm in a tower, was some form of queen?"

"Some form, yes, though her proper title was the Mistress. Horrible woman, turned me into a frog and my brother into a bear, all because she could, and she liked punishing people. Power hungry, too. She would drain any Sensitive who crossed her path to increase her power, even her own daughter, your older sister." Sir E gave a long sigh. "You were only safe because your father hid you away in this tower."

Emmazel slowly nodded. "And this Gardener?"

"Elinrose, your niece. She faced your mother five years ago and won. The Mistress thought she could drain Elin the same as any other Sensitive, but Elinrose was strong enough to take power back and gain control of the Forest instead. That was probably when you stopped dreaming of the Forest. Because it had her and was no longer calling for you."

"Oh." A shudder ran through Emmazel's body. She didn't

know what to think of this. What was she *supposed* to think of this? "And she sent you to tell me that she's not going to fight me if I'm willing to accept that she rules the Forest instead of me?"

"I know it's your rightful place," said Sir E. "But Elin is a wonderful Gardener, and the Forest loves her. I don't think you would easily dethrone her, even as powerful as you are. But you are her family, and she loves her family. She wants to reach out to you and offer sisterhood. To let you help in the Forest at her side, if you'd like. Or at least offer a truce if that's what you would prefer."

Emmazel blinked and shook her head as she tried to process this. To be told that she *should* have had power, but someone else got to it first. And now that person wanted to rub her face in it in the guise of friendship?

"Power isn't worth it, Emmazel," said Father, his voice heavy. "It destroyed your mother, and I think it would destroy you, too. You've lived your life too isolated. My own fault, I know, but I did the best I could. If this Elinrose is doing a sufficient job as the Gardener, then let her keep the Forest. You don't need it."

Emmazel shook her head again.

The two men both held their silence, thankfully, but both stared hard at her. Even when she closed her eyes closed, Emmazel still felt their gazes. Eventually, she stood and stalked away, fists tucked into her skirts as she tried to think.

"She wants peace?"

"If it's possible," said Sir E. "She understands that you're probably hurt by the loss. But, as family, she wants to try, anyway. She would at least like to send her mother, Foxglove, to see you. Your sister has missed you, even if you may have been too young to remember."

Emmazel didn't remember any life before the tower, but in her dreams about the Forest, there had been a girl she'd thought was her mother, a kind woman who always had a song to sing. Maybe this was her sister instead?

"I suppose it wouldn't hurt to meet her. Both of them. Why

didn't you tell me any of this sooner?"

"I had to be sure," said Sir E. "And then I realized that I didn't dare say a word to you about it until I had your father's permission. And he was a difficult man to find. Zephyrs are good at keeping themselves hidden."

"Right."

"But once I found a strong Sensitive who lived in a tower built by a strong Dwarven, I knew I was on the right track, especially since your name was so close to the one I sought."

"Emmazalea." The name still didn't feel like it fit. Maybe it would if she left this tower and had access to all of her power.

"Yes."

"And why did *you* come," Emmazel asked, sitting up straight. "Why did she send you instead of coming herself?"

"Because the Forest is almost a prison itself," said Father.

"In essence," Sir E agreed. "As the Gardener, Elinrose can't easily leave the Forest. Thus, as her consort, I am her liaison to the world and act on her behalf when I am away from her."

"I see." Emmazel folded her hands in her lap, then tilted her head to the side. "I'm sorry, consort? As in…"

"As in I am her husband, yes." Sir E tugged up his shirt sleeve to show off what looked like a rose vine *inked* into his skin. Similar to the ferns that wrapped around her father's arm. "I told your father that I wasn't here to pursue you as a lover; I'm a married man."

"But … but what about Heather?"

"Heather?" Sir E repeated, drawing back. "What about Heather?"

"She and you, I thought—"

"Why would you even *consider* that I was here to court her? She's your companion. I was here to gather information about you, frustrating as it was that you would always leave me to talk to her." Sir E shrugged. "But I assumed it's because you're reclusive and don't like talking about yourself."

"Emmazel has it in her head that random young lords and princes only come to her tower to marry her companions," said Father. "We can't convince her otherwise, and so Night and I figured that you would be a good object lesson. I apologize for using you, but this is a lesson she has needed to learn for a long time."

"I see." Sir E stared at Emmazel for a long moment. "Why do I keep finding myself in situations like this?" He shook his head. "I think I shall leave you to explain things to the young lady, for I have done nothing, so far as I'm aware, that could have been directly interpreted as courtship, though I now see how *you* could misconstrue it. I think I should return to the Forest now. Do you mind if I bring Elinrose and Foxglove back to visit? I think they are both eager to see you, sir, and you don't have much time left."

"I should also like to see them both," said Father. "Yes, do bring them here if you can."

"But – but what about the love potion?" blurted Emmazel.

"Love potion? What about a love potion? Did you give me one?" Sir E gave a wondering shake of his head.

"Oh, yes, but you were quite immune, young man," said Father. "What with the Forest's magic running through your veins and a *loving* marriage to the Gardener."

"I see," Sir E repeated. "Well, I think I should be off then if everything is said. I shall return, and I'm sure Elin will be better able to … explain things."

He went to the window and climbed out. Emmazel didn't even have to command the vines to let him leave. He did it himself; she felt the order.

She just sat there as the world collapsed around her. Who *was* this man to have barged in and destroyed everything she knew? A married man? Married to a woman who had stolen Emmazel's rightful throne. None of this made sense, and she had a thousand more questions.

And also an illogical idea that if she rushed after him and screamed loud enough, she could make the world fit back into her mold. That he would be a good and charming lover for Heather, the way he was supposed to be.

So she suddenly tore herself out of her chair and threw herself out of the window after him.

~

Out of the tower, Emmazel's mind exploded.

Seventy feet was a long way to fall, but vines wrapped around her and lowered her safely to the ground. Emmazel scarcely noticed over the cacophony of voices in her head.

The tower *had* suppressed her connection to the plants around her, and now they were fighting and screaming for her attention.

*Woah, there. Focus, Emmazel.*

Sir E's voice rang out louder than the trees', allowing Emmazel to fix upon it and shut out the rest.

*It's your first time out of the tower, isn't it? Take a deep breath and focus. I know the world is intimidating, but you can face it.*

Emmazel gasped and stepped back, pulling away from him. "Why couldn't you just have been the foreign prince you claimed to be!"

"Because that seemed like the right thing to lead with," said Sir E, aloud, as he laid a hand on Emmazel's arm. "It wasn't a lie. I am a prince of a country that has been cut off from this one by the Forest for the last hundred years. Elinrose's country had been cut off as well. Your mother had broken this land into pieces, and it has been my mission to help reverse her misdeeds."

"But—"

"Yes, yes, I know, you wanted me to be a good husband for your Heather, but I'm already taken, quite happily too, and I think you did need such a shock to your life."

Emmazel didn't like his words, so she shut her eyes and tried to escape. Which was difficult, given that he had his hand on her shoulder, and she couldn't seem to get her muscles to move.

But then the world shifted and bent again, and Emmazel found herself surrounded by trees, and a woman sat on a treebranch throne before her.

"Hello there. This is unexpected," said the woman. She stood and walked forward to examine Emmazel. "You're quite strong, to have brought yourself here. But, don't worry, you didn't come in body. You and I have only connected through the trees' thoughts."

"I've anchored her here," said Sir E, from behind Emmazel. The woman nodded.

"I take that you're *Mrs. E?*" asked Emmazel, trying to pull herself to her full height. Her hair was dragging in the dirt. How horrible.

The woman's eyebrow arched, and she glanced at Sir E. "You could say that. I'm the Gardener, Elinrose or Elin to my friends and family. Since you're my aunt, you're free to refer to me personally."

Emmazel drew in a breath. "I don't know you, Mrs. E. I will—"

"Elin," said Sir E, "I shall return to the Forest shortly to talk to you and explain, once I take her back to her tower so she can process everything she's learned today. It's been a very overwhelming day for her."

"Of course." A slight grin pulled at Mrs. E's mouth. "I know how disconcerting this Forest can be, especially if one finds themselves here unexpectedly. I'll help push you both home. See you soon, Earnest."

She raised her hand, the Forest faded, and Emmazel was once again standing at the foot of the tower, now with Sir E's hands on both of her shoulders.

"Back in the tower with you," he said, his voice soft. "You don't have to stay there, but you need time to adjust, I can tell. You need to go back to your sanctuary."

Emmazel opened and shut her mouth, but only a sob escaped.

"There, there," said Sir E. "Everything will be all right. It's okay to be scared when your world grows. And yours has been so small for so long."

A vine wrapped around Emmazel's waist, and then she felt her father's arms and his wind, lifting her back to the window. When in her tower, she stumbled down to her bedroom and wrapped herself up in her blankets.

She *would* get her order back. She wouldn't let this Mrs. E destroy her world.

How was she going to explain this to Heather!

# 11

"Emmazel, your father said that you're not feeling well, but there's something you need to tell me. Is everything is all right?"

Emmazel pried her eyes open and lifted the pillow from her head. "Sir E was a lying scoundrel and never cared for you at all."

Best to just say it. Let Heather know how badly Emmazel had failed her. She wished that her father hadn't already sent Heather here to interrupt her sleep.

"What?" Heather drew back, shaking her head in horror. "Are you sure? Oh, Emmazel! How horrid."

"He has a *wife*." Emmazel considered pulling the pillow back over her head. "They've been married for five years, and apparently, his wife is my *niece*.'"

"Really? Your niece? How do you have a niece?"

Emmazel let the pillow fall back on her head. "I don't know, ask my father. I don't want to talk about Mrs. E. She ruined everything."

"Well, if she was already married to him, then it can hardly be her fault," said Heather, her voice small. "But he should have told us something like that, shouldn't he? Unless…"

"As I said, he's a scoundrel of the worst sort and has sorely abused your heart, dear Heather." Emmazel sighed.

"I suppose it's just as well," Heather concluded. "I never felt right being pursued by a prince, you know. It was glorious, yes. A romantic rush – but it never felt like it was *mine*."

"I'm sorry for pushing you so hard – I should have seen through him, but I was blinded by the persona of a charming prince." Emmazel lifted the pillow from her head again and sat up. "I failed you. I don't – I don't know how this happened. I never thought there would be any other reason than courtship for a young man to seek out my tower. I knew he had likely been interested first in me, but to already be married and this! It's terrible, Heather, and I had no idea!"

A line dug between Heather's eyes as she sunk into her seat. "What is *this*? What happened, Emmazel? If you don't mind explaining, that is. I don't understand."

Emmazel opened her mouth only to release another sigh and shake her head. She rubbed her arm. "I don't walk to talk about it."

"Okay." Heather's shoulders drooped. "I'm sorry, I didn't mean to pry. I just wanted—"

"I know." Emmazel hugged the pillow. "But I don't want to talk about it. It won't help."

Talking would mean reliving, and she was trying to put that distressing experience out of her mind. Her head hurt to even *think* of how much her senses had tried to process for those few minutes she'd been out of her tower.

"I still can't believe that for as much as we talked, he never mentioned a wife." Heather collapsed back into her own thoughts and shook her head. "Unless … what's her name?"

"Mrs. E, naturally." Emmazel hugged the pillow tighter. "I mean, I think she has a name, and they said it, but I don't want to remember it. I'm sorry, Heather, but yesterday was horrible, and I shut out much of it."

"He mostly told stories about himself and his older brother as they grew up," Heather continued. "There was a girl named Lilly that he was *supposed* to marry, but they didn't love each other, so he let her marry the man she did love. But he didn't say anything about *him* marrying someone else after that."

"Well, he wasn't sure if my father would want me to find out about his wife. My niece." Emmazel squeezed her eyes shut. "My head still hurts."

"Oh? I'm so sorry – what happened?" asked Heather, leaning forward to lay a hand on Emmazel's arm.

"I went outside. The stone of my tower really does keep things quiet. And I had no idea…"

She never wanted to leave her tower again. Emmazel knew that beyond any doubt. Yet, if Sir E was to return with his wife, Emmazel's niece, the woman who had taken what should have been Emmazel's throne, then she couldn't appear weak before Mrs. E.

"I don't know what we're going to do." Emmazel shook her head. "Because he might be gone now, but he's going to come back and bring her with him this time."

"Oh no!"

"I know." Emmazel rocked forward. "But my father has already approved her visit, so there's nothing we can do. She's family, after all."

"It's hard to think of."

"He came looking for me on *her* behalf," Emmazel explained. "So, it's not a case of 'what are the chances?' It's a 'How could I be so stupid?' But I live in a tower, I don't know anything about the world, you have been sheltered and unloved, and it just turned out all wrong."

"It could have been worse," said Heather. "We'll just have to be more careful in the future. And, Emmazel, remember that I'm here to be *your* companion. I don't have to find love. If a life without a husband is good enough for you, then it's good enough for me, too."

She stood and left before Emmazel could argue, and so Emmazel sat on the bed, feeling horrible. This wasn't how this was supposed to happen at all. Heather deserved happiness, not to share Emmazel's prison.

~

"I heard you're awake. How are you feeling? Did you enjoy

your little excursion outside, Emmazel? Have you realized how little you actually know?"

Emmazel glared as Night stalked into her room and perched at the foot of her bed. "I'm holding you responsible for this *misunderstanding*."

"Oh?" Night licked his paw. "Was I the one who convinced my companion to abandon her better sense and pine after a prince, against my best friend's advice?"

"You're calling yourself my best friend? I'm not feeling so generous right now."

"What other friends do you have? And don't say Heather, after how badly you've abused her heart."

Emmazel pursed her lips and flopped back against the bed. "Oh, I don't know. Berry might be my best friend right now. She might be entirely too obsessed with Kendra Flaxseed, but at least she almost only ever has *nice* things to tell me when she visits. And I'm who she chooses to visit in her *free* time. She isn't trapped in this tower with me."

"No need to say such horrible things," said Night, jumping onto her blankets. "And don't worry – I'm not trapped in this tower, either. I *choose* to stay here."

"Right. Of course." Emmazel tugged the blankets up to her chin, knocking him off of his feet. "Did my father tell you to not tell me that Sir E was already married? Because you should have told me, either way. You should have seen Heather's face when I told her!"

"I wish I could have seen your face," said Night. "I told you to not encourage her, and she wouldn't have even considered trying to attract his attention if you hadn't put the thought in her head. She'll recover, though, if she's been able to recover from Farmer Marrin."

"Oh, do you really think that she cared so much about *him*?" Emmazel glanced at Night out of the corner of her eye.

"At least as much she ever did Earnest," said Night, licking his paw again. "And since Farmer Marrin is now courting Betsy Miller, I'm afraid you entirely ruined that chance for her."

"I'm still sure she can do better than a farmer," said

Emmazel. "Stop looking so smug. You're still a talking cat who's too scared to speak to her."

"Emma…" Night lowered his paw.

"Don't give me those eyes – you deserve that. Do you know how awkward it is for me to sit in silence with you because you refuse to let someone I *live* with know that you can talk? If I'm going to be stuck with her instead of marrying her off the way I had expected, then I can't keep this up. I respect your privacy, Night, but this is ridiculous! She knows I speak to plants – she can speak to plants herself! She *won't* find you strange."

Night stared at Emmazel, and she thought he might leave again to avoid her pushing. Then he settled down and laid his head on his paws. "We're not ready yet, I told you. But … I'll try to stay away when you and Heather are together."

"You already *do* that!" Emmazel rolled her eyes. "You're *such* a frustrating cat, you know."

"I try my best." Night slowly blinked. "Now, your father sent me to ask if you have any other questions. You need to put your mind to rest if you're to recover."

Emmazel sighed. "I suppose you knew from the start exactly who he was and who he was married to, and you were the one who told him to tell me nothing."

"I did," said Night. "I wanted to tell him nothing at all, but as the Gardener's husband, I couldn't deny him, and he was determined to meet you."

"I will assume the reason you couldn't deny him is one of the things you can't talk about."

"You would be correct."

"Then I won't ask. Annoying you might be, I would hate to lose one of my few companions, especially not the most loyal."

Night gave a quiet purr. "I'm glad you appreciate my merits."

"I still haven't forgiven you yet." Emmazel huffed. "Why did Sir E call me Emmazalea? Why have I never heard that name?"

"Emmazel is enough of a mouthful," said Night. "But Sir E is correct. Emmazalea is your real name. The name your mother gave you. Your father wanted you to be free from her legacy, and so he cut it short."

Emmazel pursed her lips. "And my mother ruled a Forest?"

"Your mother was the Mistress, the most powerful Sensitive in the land, with the power of the Forest itself as well," said Night. "But the power corrupted her, or perhaps she was always a little too bitter. She was a cruel woman. I don't know how your father became her consort or if they ever loved each other, but he fled here with you when she decided you were a threat to her power. As her more powerful daughter, you should have been her heir, but she refused to give up her place."

"But then this Gardener…"

"Your father was just wondering if you might be ready to face your mother, but then he felt her power break," said Night. "If someone else had taken care of the Mistress, he was willing to let her establish her reign unhindered."

"Did he even care what *I* wanted?" Emmazel shifted her glare to the wall.

"Less than I think he should," said Night, climbing into her lap. "Your father has always been far more concerned with keeping you safe. I think … I think he might be scared of any desire you might express. Scared that you're more like your mother than he can bear. And so it's easier to keep you in a tower and keep you ignorant."

Emmazel scratched him behind the ears. "And now that I know, what will happen?"

"For now, please just carry on as you always have. Earnest will return with the Gardener, and you can make decisions once you've spoken with her. With your mother dead, your father won't survive her much longer, and you will need to find your own place after he's gone. Since her consort reports that she is favorable to you and is willing to take you as an ally, you don't have to stay contained in the tower if you don't want to."

"I don't think I'm made for the outside world. I've lived in this tower for too long."

Night gave a long sigh. "Perhaps so, Emmazel, but perhaps

you only need time to learn and adjust. You're a smart young woman. I don't think you should stay in a tower your whole life."

Emmazel took a deep breath and hugged him to her chest. "I don't know. I don't even know if I ever even *want* to leave the tower again."

"I can't say that I blame you, and if you choose to be as cowardly as your father, so be it."

"I hate you."

"So you keep saying."

*12* Emmazel managed to pry herself from bed the next morning and went upstairs to her garden for a bit of peace. Yet, the room didn't seem to provide the sanctuary it normally did.

After hearing the full voices of the trees outside, her herbs and shrubs were muffled, and she could hear how *wrong* it was. And trying to speak to the plants was like, well, trying to throw her thoughts through a stone wall.

Be that as it may, she still gave her tiny garden the attention it deserved before she fled back downstairs and threw herself into her chair, hands pressed to the sides of her head. A garden didn't belong at the top of a tower. She knew that. She'd always known that. But she was trapped up here, and it was trapped here with her.

What was she supposed to do? Her life had been ripped open. She couldn't bear to go outside again, but she now felt how small and artificial her tower was.

Inside, she felt like she would choke; outside, it was as though she would shatter into a thousand pieces.

She couldn't move forward, and neither could she bear to go back, and so instead, she just sat there with her hands over her ears, trying to wish the whole world away.

"Emmazel, there's someone calling you outside, do you hear?"

Emmazel sat up and dropped her hands from her ears as she blinked at Heather. "What?"

"Someone is calling your name outside, but I don't recognize them." Heather nodded at the window. "Two women."

Emmazel unfolded and went to the window, bracing herself for the outside world – though it seemed as quiet as ever. Sure enough, two women stood below – Anna was one of them, but Emmazel didn't recognize the other, either.

But, any friend of Anna's was sure to be a friend of hers, and she was desperate for an outside voice.

She wondered that she'd never noticed how much easier it was to instruct the vines in the window – vines that were technically outside. The herbs upstairs would never move like the vines would.

"I'm sorry, I was distracted," she said as she helped Anna climb into the room. The second woman seemed vaguely familiar up close, but Emmazel still didn't know her. "I had a horrid shock the other day, and I've been out of sorts since."

"I'm so sorry." Anna paused to pat Emmazel's cheek. "I hope you're recovering."

Emmazel shrugged. "I'm glad to see you."

"Of course, child!" Anna drew back with a smile. "Lady Isolde was visiting, and I just *had* to bring her here to see you. And I'm glad I did if you're so distressed!"

Emmazel blinked as she focused again on the other woman. "Isolde! It's been too long!"

Isolde had been her first companion. She had married a lower noble who had been the first to find their tower. He had been far too enamored with Emmazel, convinced she was a damsel in distress. She was only too grateful when Isolde confessed an attraction to the man, though it had taken a love potion to shift his attention entirely.

"You said it would be best if I kept Lord John as far away from you as possible, and so I have done just that," said Isolde, dipping into a curtsey. "But when I paid Lady Anna a visit and she told me of her visit to you, I must confess that the thought of seeing you again was more than I could resist! Oh, but you're looking well, old friend – scarcely a day older than when I left you!"

Emmazel gave a thin-lipped smile and shrugged. "I have been blessed by youth. You're looking well yourself, I promise. The years have been kind to you."

Isolde's dark hair was now lightened by strands of gray, lines creased the corners of her eyes, and her slim figure was long gone, but after twenty-five years, Emmazel knew she could hardly expect the same nineteen-year-old girl to stand before her now.

"I hope Lord John has treated you well?"

"As well as could be expected, for the way it began," Isolde answered. "I gave him an heir, a spare, and three daughters to make alliances with, and he lets me wear fine dresses and host parties for my friends. I've had a better life than an orphan like myself should have hoped for, and I will always be grateful that you gave me the opportunity. If you have ever felt a crumb of guilt, don't, my friend, though I will confess that I am quite aware of how many of your companions shared my fate in the years since!"

"Oh, every one of us wanted it just as you ever did, and I assure you we've been just as happy," said Anna. She tilted her head to the side as she noticed Heather. "And you must be Emmazel's latest companion. She said you already have a young man courting you. How is that going? Is he the most charming gentleman ever?"

Heather's eyes went wide, and she glanced to Emmazel for help as she stepped back.

"Sir E proved to already be married and here only to satisfy his curiosity about me," said Emmazel. "Thus the shock we suffered."

"Oh! You poor thing!" Anna rushed forward to wrap Heather up in a hug. "That must have been such a disappointment!"

"I'll recover," said Heather. "It never felt *right* after all. I'm glad it's over."

"And another gentleman will come along – they always do," said Isolde. "And you're still young and beautiful. You have time."

Heather's nose wrinkled, and she burrowed into the hug. "But do I really need love to be happy? Emmazel is just fine on her own."

Anna huffed and gave Heather an extra squeeze. "Don't use Emmazel as your measure of happiness. She lives in a tower and makes love potions."

"Maybe she can teach me."

"It's too soon for you to make decisions about love," said Emmazel, putting a hand on Heather's shoulder. "One should never swear off men until at least six weeks have passed since your disappointment. Give it time."

"And at what point in your life in a tower did you learn that piece of wisdom?" asked Isolde.

Emmazel straightened and lifted her chin. "My father has brought me at least three companions who were fresh off of a romantic disappointment, and *they* still found love in the end." She shrugged. "I'm not saying that you should throw yourself at another young man immediately, but … don't give up. Love can still find you."

~

Anna and Isolde stayed for hours, and Emmazel drank up every moment of it. She'd missed her oldest friend, and she'd worried over her fate. Isolde had even predated Night, as the annoying cat had only come to live in the tower about two years after her marriage.

Learning that her oldest friend's life *had* been better for her influence did Emmazel a world of good, and she felt her spirits rise which each passing minute.

All too soon, though, it was time for Anna and Isolde to leave, and Emmazel hugged them both tightly before giving instructions to the vines. If she hugged Isolde a bit tighter and shed a few more tears over her, then no one could blame her.

"I'll try to bring her again before her visit is over," Anna promised. "And I'll be sure to return. Oh! But I do really think that Prince Christian will come soon, and how will you like that? Keep your chin high because you *are* a clever young woman and you certainly have much to offer the world."

"Well, first, I would have to leave my tower," Emmazel answered with a heavy sigh.

And then she and Heather were left alone again. Emmazel threw herself back down into her chair and frowned at her companion.

"I have lived in this tower for decades, and I've had thirty-two companions before you, and I've seen almost every one of them happily married. There were two who chose to not pursue the relationship after they left me, but they're still happy with the life they chose. You, Heather, have been my first failure, and for that, I apologize profusely."

Heather's eyes went wide as she glanced out the window. "Oh, Emmazel, you don't have to. You did the best you could. How could you have known that he was married? I didn't know, and I talked to him far more than you did!"

"Yes, but you would never have considered him romantically if I hadn't encouraged you," said Emmazel. "I meddled. I pushed my opinions onto you and didn't let you think for yourself."

Heather chewed her lip as she shifted her weight from one foot to the other. Then she shrugged. "You wanted me to have the happily-ever-after you can't have," she said. "It might have ended badly, but I appreciate what you're trying to do."

Emmazel shook her head. "That still doesn't make it right. But … you're correct. I was trying to give you what I can't have myself. Because I see so much of me in you — two lost girls who don't know where they fit in the world, and we each want to give so much."

"What are we going to do?"

"I don't know, but you shouldn't give up on love, as I told you." Emmazel took a deep breath. "This tower is my prison, not yours. You deserve so much more, and don't let my mistakes make you give up."

Heather stood with her eyes downcast as she considered. "I agree that swearing off romance completely would be foolish, but I'm not going to go looking for love. I think that will only lead to disappointment."

Emmazel nodded. "And I promise to never again try to influence you one way or another. Your heart is yours to follow. If … if you should like to share that you *have* fallen in love again, you can, but there should be no names unless it's a set and sure thing!"

"I don't think all *that* is necessary." The line between Heather's eyes deepened.

"I assure you it is. I'm afraid I just can't keep myself from meddling, otherwise, and you deserve to make your own decisions. You've been passed about for too long." Emmazel gave Heather a reassuring smile. "And, don't worry – you're a beautiful young lady and are sure to catch some other young man's eye. And if you ever do need another love potion … well, I still know how to mix them."

"I don't want to force anything, but … thank you. I know you're just trying to help the best way you know."

It was Emmazel's turn to crinkle her nose in a frown. "If you need them," she repeated.

Heather took a deep breath and nodded. "Right."

Emmazel leaned back in her seat, rubbing her temples. "I can't stay in this tower my whole life, can I?"

"I mean, you can, I'm sure. You've gone this far." Heather's frown grew as she glanced towards the window. "But I think, if you don't want to stay here, you shouldn't have to."

"I'm here for my protection, but it seems that I don't need protecting anymore," Emmazel mused. "It was more than I could bear when I went outside two days ago, but maybe I can grow used to it."

"I don't know how you can stand to be in this tower all the time, though I've told you that already."

"Now that I've been outside, I don't know either. It's so quiet in here." Emmazel sighed. "I don't know how this tower blocks everything out, but it feels wrong. And I don't want to be wrong."

"Do you think your father would let you leave this tower again?"

Emmazel lifted her chin. "I would like to see him try to stop me."

# 13

Leaving the tower again was easier said than done. Emmazel sat in her tower window, staring down at the ground below as she ran her braid through her hands.

"It's not that bad – the vines will keep you from falling," Heather said behind her. "Don't forget that."

Emmazel spared Heather a glare for the cheek. "I think it must be easier to climb the tower than it is to descend. It's a long way down, you know."

"How *did* you leave, when you left?" Heather folded her arms over her chest. "Because you're acting like this *is* your first time."

"I jumped."

Heather made a choking noise. "You *jumped?*"

Emmazel shrugged and leaned against the window frame. "I was rather focused on Sir E's betrayal and didn't think."

"Well, don't jump this time," Heather advised. "If it'll help, just close your eyes and let the vines lower you to the ground. That's what works for me."

"Are you sure that I should do this now? It grows late – perhaps we should go make supper and save this for tomorrow," said Emmazel. "Father should be home again soon, and what will he say if he finds us here without having finished dinner."

Heather didn't answer and continued to stare at Emmazel with her arms crossed over her chest.

"You are intimidating when you stare at people like that, did you know?"

"I have to get the children to mind *somehow*," said Heather. "And you're still stalling. I know you're scared of leaving your tower, but if you want to experience the world outside, you can't put it off forever."

Emmazel chewed her lip as she stared down at the ground below. She knew Heather was right – it was advice she had herself given many times. Still.

"So, you're treating me like a child?"

"You're acting like a child," Heather answered, and Emmazel heard a frown enter her voice. "How old *are* you, anyway? Because you've been in this tower for longer than I can remember."

Emmazel shrugged. "I'm not sure. It's not something my father cares about, so I've never been able to keep careful track of the passing of time. I'm about of an age with Isolde, though, and she's in her late forties."

"Well, for a woman in your forties, you're certainly not acting like it."

"I don't even *look* it." Emmazel chewed her lip. "Maybe this is a foolish idea. The world outside will never accept me for who I am."

"That doesn't mean you must stay in this tower unhappy forever," said Heather. "You deserve to exist in the world just as much as anyone else does."

"I can exist in this tower just fine. I have for this long!"

"Oh, just get *on* with it!"

And before Emmazel could turn or even think to protest, Heather shoved her out of the window.

~

The tumble *was* decidedly less of a shock than her jump from the window. It took only a thought for the vines to wrap around her and slow her descent.

She was still several feet away from the ground when she finally stopped, clinging to the side of the tower. Slowly, she caught her breath, staring at the grass beneath her as she tried to process what had just happened. Finally, she looked up to find Heather leaning out of the window, staring down at her.

"You pushed me!" she shouted up.

"I … I know!" Heather sounded as shocked as Emmazel. They stayed there a moment more, staring at each other, before she added, "Well, are you going to go the rest of the way?"

Emmazel looked back down at the ground and took a shaky breath. "This is a really good first step. I don't think it's strictly *necessary* to actually touch the ground. I could go back up now…"

"I think you shouldn't turn back when you've made it this far already," Heather answered. "You're so close! You can do it! Just a little bit further!"

"You're patronizing me, and it's strange."

"Sorry!" And Heather sounded genuinely remorseful. "But you're still stalling, and it was your decision to go outside."

"Right, right."

Emmazel took a deep breath and asked the vines to lower her the rest of the way to the ground.

It wasn't *nearly* as loud this time as it had been when she chased Sir E out of the tower. The soil beneath her feet was soft and inviting, and the grass and trees buzzed with a quiet song.

"*This* is right," she muttered. "This is the world as it should be."

And now how would she force herself back into the tower? How could she let the world go quiet again?

Torture. Pure torture.

"See, it's not so bad, now is it?"

Emmazel turned as Heather stepped onto the ground beside her. "No. No, it isn't, and I think this is what worried me the most. It's what worried my father, I'm sure. The fact that I might *like* it out here."

"And you *do* like it?" Heather's voice was too smug. Of

course, she didn't know the gravity of the situation.

Emmazel chewed her lip as she pondered how to answer. How to explain what she didn't fully understand?

"If you want a flower to thrive, you don't put it in a stone box."

"Oh."

"That tower was to protect me from my mother, who was apparently power-hungry and wouldn't even have had compassion for her own daughter." Emmazel glanced up at the tower. It seemed so much taller out here! "But she's been gone for five years, and he still didn't even think about letting me leave – never even told me it was an option! And, yes, he says he was worried that my niece would see me as a rival, but I think he worried more that *I* would object to her theft of my throne."

"*Your* throne?"

"I couldn't claim it myself from inside this tower," said Emmazel. "But I should have a chance. My father kept that from me."

"So, what are you going to do?" asked Heather. "And are you *sure* that your father trusts you so little?"

"I think my father is a fearful man," said Emmazel. "He was clearly hurt by my mother's wickedness, and he projects those fears onto me. That isn't to say that he doesn't love me – I don't think such a thing at all – but it's hard to love properly when one has been hurt as badly as he has been."

"I think I understand," said Heather.

"I think you might," said Emmazel, "for you've been hurt, too, and you don't hold it against anyone. I still love my father, despite all of his flaws. This Mrs. E, however…"

"Do you think that she'll take issue with you?" Heather wrung her hands.

"I don't know. I don't know her." Emmazel twisted away from the tower. She didn't know what direction Mrs. E might be and so fixed her gaze on some indeterminate point on the horizon. "I know I'm not prepared to love her, not when she has stolen what should have been mine. Maybe she only took this throne because I didn't know it was mine to claim, but it was still my right, and she has taken it. She is coming, and I will greet her with all civility, for let it not be said that Emmazalea is an ungracious host. She is family, after all."

The longer name seemed to fit better now that she was outside. Now that there was room for *her* to be bigger. Emmazel closed her eyes and reached out to the plants and trees around her. They practically buzzed with excitement at the contact, ready to jump into action at her bidding.

"I will need to move my garden out here. And decide what I'm going to tell my father. Should we throw a party to welcome Mrs. E? I feel that we should host a party! Let her see that I'm no sheltered child who has lived in a tower my whole life!"

"You … have lived in a tower your whole life, though."

"But I am not *ignorant*," Emmazel insisted.

Heather tilted her head to the side and abandoned the argument. "What sort of party do you plan to throw."

"I … I don't know. I've never been to a party myself, so I don't know what to do with one. Perhaps I should ask Anna. I'm sure she would be willing to help."

"I've never been to a party, either, so I think asking Anna would be a good idea, though she's already left, and we don't know when she'll return."

"I'll send a letter," said Emmazel. "Do you know how to send a letter? Or maybe she'll return sooner than later – Isolde wants to see me again before she leaves, after all."

"That might work, then," said Heather. "Because I don't know how to send a letter. It's more expensive than I could ever afford, and I didn't have anyone to write, anyway."

"Neither have I," said Emmazel. "Not even my former companions."

She frowned. Did she really let these women drift out of her life so easily? Maybe Night had been right to criticize the way she treated them.

"Are you ready to go back in yet?" asked Heather. "Because it is time to be fixing dinner, before your father returns home."

"You can go on ahead," said Emmazel, waving a hand towards the tower. "I'll follow shortly."

"All right," said Heather, and Emmazel heard her give a quiet order for the vines to let her back into the tower, and she felt a surge of pride in her friend. In her confusion, Emmazel had not noticed that Heather had been letting herself into the tower, and she was glad to realize that the girl had been practicing.

Emmazel focused again on the song of the plants around herself. It was so rich and pure. It filled the air and made the world feel complete, leaving her at peace for, perhaps, the first time in her life.

She closed her eyes and sat down, running a hand through the grass.

How had she ever feared this? How had she ever lived peacefully within the tower's walls?

"What have we here? Did you fall out of the tower again? Do you finally realize how difficult it is to come and go from the tower without the help of your lovely braid?"

Emmazel opened her eyes, but not even Night's snark was enough to destroy her good humor, right now.

"Heather pushed me, actually, and I haven't yet gathered the wherewithal to ask the vines to take me back inside." She gave a careless shrug. He hadn't *really* criticized her location, so she wasn't going to defend herself yet.

Night paused with a paw in the air. "She *pushed* you?" he repeated.

"I was taking too much time deciding to descend on my own, and I suppose she grew impatient. The dear girl is growing so confident – I'm proud of her, Night, I really am."

"I see." Night gave the airborne paw an indignant lick and swiped at his ears. "Well, if you're feeling better out here than you did the last time, I don't see the harm in it. Your father might throw a fit if he saw you, but you're growing up, and the world is changing. It's time that you had a bit of freedom and you learned to integrate."

"You don't think that I shall destroy the world with my

mastery over plants?" asked Emmazel, raising an eyebrow.

Night lashed his tail back and forth in his version of a shrug. "I trust you to know better than that. You have a good heart, for all your flaws. Just remember that you don't, in fact, know best, and all will be well."

"Right." Emmazel frowned.

"Of course, you will need to decide what to do about your father," Night continued. "I know he won't be happy to learn that you overcame your fear of the outside. Will you hide this from him? Will you try to convince him that this is best, after all? Or are you willing to give it up to please him? You won't have him for much longer, and I don't think you want to waste his last days arguing."

Emmazel inhaled sharply and rubbed her arms. "I – I don't know." The thought of hiding something like *this* from her father felt so wrong, but would he understand? Could she give this up and endure the stone walls if it would bring him peace?

"I don't think Mrs. E would like to enter the Tower," she finally said. "And if I'm to meet her, I can't hide. I'd like to plan a party to welcome her – I don't know how yet, but it feels like the right thing to do. I think, if I have everything in place before he finds out, then he won't be able to tell me no."

"So you mean to trick him into giving permission?"

"I don't *need* permission." Emmazel bristled. "I'm an adult, and it's time for me to do things on my own. I need him to see that."

"Good luck with that," said Night, after a long moment, and, surprisingly, there was no snark in this voice but true encouragement. "I will see what I can do to soften his heart. I think he listens to me."

Emmazel nodded. "Thank you."

"You know I only want the best for you, and I have never believed that keeping you trapped in the tower was what was best. It was merely what was necessary to keep you safe from your mother." Night lashed his tale again. "Now, will you do the thing you do with the vines to let us inside? Because you know I have as yet to learn how to do it for myself. I just don't think I'm made the same as you and Heather. Clever girl, Heather. Isn't she the first to figure it out on her own?"

Emmazel gave a small smile. "Yes, she is." She stared up at the tower window. "I don't want to go back inside, but I suppose I have to. Let's go."

# 14

Their plans to talk to Anna about the party changed when Berry flew into the window the next morning as Emmazel was hauling her plant pots down the stairs. They couldn't stay inside a moment longer, and if her plants were outside, then there would be no reason for her father to tell her she couldn't join them, right?

"Oh! Oh! Oh!" cried the fairy, zooming around Emmazel's head. "Are you rearranging? I've never seen you rearrange before!"

"Gardens don't belong inside, so I'm taking mine outside," Emmazel explained, glancing at the fairy out of the corner of her eye.

"Oh! Oh!" Really, did Berry know *any* other word? "But I thought that you can't go outside. That's why I have to come visit you."

"Yes," said Emmazel. "That's how it's always been, but now I've gone outside and survived the experience, so why am I keeping my plants inside?"

"Right, right, of course," said Berry, flitting back and forth.

"So, what does Kendra's letter say today?" Emmazel asked. It was best to get this over with and done. She had things to do today and couldn't waste all of her time listening to the fairy.

"Oh! No! No letter today – Kendra's come home herself, and I wanted to come tell you the news!" Berry clapped her hands. "I know how much you love her letters, so I came to ask if you would like me to bring *her* here. I know you don't take visitors, but she's such a dear girl, and the two of you would be *such* friends. She needs some friends here, she's missing Lady Camilla so much."

"What?" Emmazel stood straight and blinked at the fairy.

"I could go back and get her right now if you would like," Berry offered. "She says she doesn't have any plans for today, so I told her I could introduce her to a friend. I didn't tell her it was you. I probably should have. But I wanted to make *sure* that I could bring her here."

Emmazel blinked more as she continued to stare at Berry. She had never even *considered* bringing in someone from the outside world as a *visitor,* especially not someone that her father hadn't chosen as her companion.

There wasn't a bone in her body that actually wanted to meet Kendra – not with how *perfect* she was in Berry's mind. But Emmazel was also in a rebellious mood, and she wanted to test the limits of her world. She needed to practice her social skills before meeting Mrs. E.

"Perhaps you can take Heather and me to go visit *her,*" she suggested.

"Oh? But that would mean leaving your tower, and you don't leave your tower. Your father…"

"I've left my tower before, and I'd like to learn how to live in the world outside. My niece is coming to visit, and I'm going to throw her a party."

"Oh! Oh! A party!" Berry was flittering around again. "How delightful! I didn't know you had a niece!"

"Neither did I," said Emmazel, turning back to the lavender pot she was hauling down the stairs. "She's Sir E's husband, actually. You know, the gentleman who was staying with your Flaxseeds."

"Oh, she's Earnest's wife? Ah, the dear girl – he speaks well of her – you must be so eager to meet her."

"Yes," said Emmazel, and she didn't elaborate. No need to *attempt* to explain the whole convoluted mess to the simple-minded fairy. Berry would never understand.

"Oh, to think that we had someone so close to you under our very roof! Did he know? I wonder why he never said anything about it."

"He was respecting my father's secrecy, I think," Emmazel explained. "He didn't say anything to me about it, either, not until he had to."

"Oh. Oh. Oh."

Emmazel took a nerve-steadying breath so she wouldn't roll her eyes. "So, should I tell Heather that we're going into the village? I'm sure it doesn't take long to get ready, but we are in the middle of things." She hauled the lavender pot the last few feet to the window and hefted it up so the vines could wrap around it and lower it to the ground. Heather was at the bottom to tuck it away.

Simple as that.

"Ah, yes, you are, indeed," said Berry. She flitted back and forth thoughtfully. "I could still go get her and bring her here. I won't take you away from what you're doing, and she can use the exercise."

"I could use the exercise, too!" Emmazel argued. She didn't know *why* she wanted this so much, but she couldn't lose an argument with a fairy.

"Then you can come to see her tomorrow after her visit today – I'm sure you'll soon be the best of friends!"

And with that, Berry darted out of the window and was gone.

Emmazel gave a long sigh and headed back up the stairs to retrieve the next plant. She'd tried, but had forgotten that arguing with a fairy was pointless, because they only had enough space in their head for their own ideas.

And now Kendra was going to come here, to her domain, and there was nothing she could do about it, any more than she could prevent Mrs. E's approach.

How had her life spun so wildly out of control?

Oh, yes, that was right – Mrs. E took Emmazel's throne and sent all of the carefully collected pieces of her life spinning wildly out of control.

She marched back up the stairs and wrapped her arms around the pot holding her rose vine. She still had most of her plants to move outside. She couldn't sit here crippled by the loss of control. Who knew when her father would come home and ask questions?

~

She had moved her rose, onions, and laurel tree outside by the time Berry returned with Kendra trailing hesitantly behind her. Emmazel had never seen her in person, so she hurried down the vines herself as she saw the young woman crest the hill with the fairy darting around her.

Kendra was a elegant young woman with dark hair and eyes, wearing a sensible blue walking dress. She drew up short as she neared the tower and narrowed a suspicious glare on Emmazel before she turned to the fairy.

"You didn't say that you were taking me to the witch of the tower."

Emmazel drew up straight and narrowed her own eyes at the name. Of *course,* Kendra would buy into that hateful title. It was just the sort of thing she would believe.

But … she needed to convince the people of Hightower that it was nothing but a fabrication if she was going to integrate into society. Getting angry about the name was merely a good way to prove it.

"Oh! Oh! But Emmazel is nice! She listens to all of your letters and thinks of you as the friend she's never had," Berry explained. "And now she's planning a party to celebrate her niece's visit, but she's never planned a party before and needs help."

"I see," said Kendra, her lips pinched together. She turned back to stare at Emmazel, sparing a glance towards Heather. "I take it that this is your most recent companion. Have you not found *her* a noble husband yet? I thought you couldn't leave your tower."

Her voice was so polite it was nearly emotionless. Emmazel

sensed that there were sharp barbs threaded through it. She couldn't answer them, though. She had to stay polite.

This wasn't an argument with Night, she had to remind herself.

"I learned that I have gained a reputation of being a witch and decided that I ought to do what I can to dispel it. Staying inside a tower at all times doesn't do much to dispel such a rumor."

Kendra slowly blinked. "I see."

"And, yes, Heather is my companion, and no, there has been no young noble who has won her heart, nor am I in any sort of rush to get rid of her. As my companion, she's a dear friend, after all."

"I see."

"Oh, the two of you will be *such* friends," Berry declared, utterly oblivious to the tension between the women.

"I take it you must be Kendra," said Heather, stepping forward to offer a placating smile. "I think I saw you around the village before you left to become a lady's maid. We never talked, though. I don't think you would have ever even noticed the orphan girl who stayed with the blacksmith."

"I see." Kendra's lips pinched tighter while she glanced back to Berry. "And you've been reading her my letters?"

"Oh, yes, and she loves them so much!" Berry insisted. "So, will you help her with her party? She's lived in a tower all her life and doesn't know how to throw one, and that's such a shame!"

"I suppose it is," said Kendra. She glanced up at the tower window. "I won't go inside that tower, but I shall do what I can. I need the distraction."

"Oh? Is everything all right?" Emmazel stepped forward as she heard a small crack in Kendra's voice.

Kendra turned an icy glare back to her. "I just have little to do at home, you know. My parents are pressuring me to let them throw me a welcome home party, and I think your niece would be as good an excuse to allow it as any. When did you say she's coming?"

"I'm … not sure, actually," Emmazel confessed, glancing down. "Her husband left a few days ago saying he would bring her back, but that's all I know."

"Earnest said that he would bring his wife and family back in a few weeks," Berry supplied. "So … in a few weeks."

"Fair enough." Kendra gave a slow nod. "And will you be able to come to my home for the party, or will we need to hold it here? Because if my parents throw it, I don't think they will be happy to hold it here."

"I think your house will be fine," said Emmazel. She didn't want to surrender so much control over the party, but she didn't know how to throw one. And if she was offered help, she would be a fool to not take it, even if she might receive better help later. She didn't know when Anna would visit again, after all.

"Good, because I didn't know how I would be able to convince them to throw it here." Kendra took a deep breath and shifted awkwardly. "So, would you like to come home with me now to plan, or would you prefer to come tomorrow? You seem to be in the middle of … something."

"I can bring Emmazel to visit you tomorrow," Heather offered. "I know the way. And we're in the middle of moving her garden outside. If you'd like to help with that, I'm sure you can. Except you don't seem to want to go into the tower…"

"No, I would much prefer to stay on the ground," Kendra said. "But … if there is something out here you'll let me do, I would be more than willing."

"You can help Heather move the pots into place down here," said Emmazel. She hadn't expected Kendra to be so willing, but maybe she shouldn't have been surprised. Kendra was, after all, determined to be gracious and helpful whenever possible – that's something she said so *very* often in her letters. And she was looking for a reason to be away from home. Emmazel didn't know why she had come home if there was such clear tension between her and her parents, but what did she know? She lived in a tower.

And she needed to get her plants outside before her father

came home. She had her own domestic tension to worry about.

**15** Hightower's streets were frightful. So many people were jostling together, everyone trying to fill the same space, and Emmazel didn't know how anyone could stand it.

Heather's hand wrapped around her wrist, and the young girl offered Emmazel an encouraging smile. "It's not nearly as bad as market day," she explained. "You're doing fine for your first day out. Now come on."

Emmazel's head whipped back and forth as Heather tugged her through the crowd. There was just so much to see and absorb. So many people. She would have never guessed that so many could be in just one place.

"And we're just in a village," she muttered. "What would it be like in a city?"

"I don't want to even think about that," said Heather, shaking her head. "Maybe you can ask Kendra all about cities. She's been to them, and would likely love to tell you all about them."

Kendra probably would. Satisfy her self-satisfaction in how much better she was than Emmazel. Make herself feel so much more superior.

Emmazel banished that thought. It wasn't kind, and she was trying to be grateful that Kendra was helping. After all, she only knew Emmazel's reputation as the witch of the tower. And here she was, still helping. Yes, it was because Berry had pressured her, but it was still her decision.

Emmazel focused again on the people around her. The women were familiar enough - she'd had her string of companions to compare and contrast against each other - but the men and children! Her father was the only man she really knew, and she'd never seen a child, not since she and Isolde had grown. They came in all shapes and sizes, and many stared at Emmazel and her long braid with shameless wide eyes.

She was glad that she had taken Heather's suggestion to loop her braid today, so the bottom of the loop only hung to her knees and the end of her hair was safely tucked up at the nape of her neck. If she was going to be going outside like this, she would likely need to cut her hair entirely, but she hadn't *quite* brought herself to make that great of a change. She'd been growing her hair her whole life, and it was something she could cling to as the rest of her world changed.

The crowd was thinning now as Heather and Emmazel walked up a hill. Emmazel had no idea that so much walking could be required to get from one place to another, and this hill was a new torture. Even moving her plants downstairs had been less exertion than this.

"Here we are," Heather announced, her voice dropping to an awed whisper. Now they stood in front of a massive gate. It wasn't nearly as tall as Emmazel's tower, but the walls stretched away from them and down the hill, and Emmazel had never seen such a sprawling building.

But, then, the tower *had* been the only building she'd ever seen.

It was made of stone, and she wondered if it would suppress her connection to the plants the same way the tower did. Heather stepped forward and knocked. It was a few minutes before a small wooden door opened beside the heavy wooden gate, and a little man who appeared as old as Emmazel's own father emerged.

"Hello there, we're here to see Kendra, if we can?" said Heather, dipping into a small curtsey. "She said we could come see her today."

"Of course, of course," said the old man. "Follow me. Miss Kendra is waiting for you in the parlor."

Emmazel braced herself as she and Heather followed him through the doorway, but she didn't feel the silence of the tower press upon her. She was further from the plants, but she could still hear them as well as ever.

Once through the gate, they entered a massive house and wound their way through hallways until they arrived in a frankly massive room where Kendra sat, arranging a vase of flowers.

"You're here," she said, raising an eyebrow as she entered the room. "I wasn't sure that you would be so serious and leave your fortress."

"The one I hid from no longer lives," said Emmazel. "So, how do we plan a party?"

Kendra set the vase to the side and stood, a frown momentarily flickering across her placid face. "Yes, that is why you've come, isn't it? Well, let's begin; there's no use sitting about when there's work to be done. My parents are more than willing to host the party for you - it seems that your niece's husband has made a favorable impression on them. And they are quite intrigued by her relation to you."

"I think we all are," said Heather. "It was ... quite unexpected. Who knew that Emmazel even had a niece?"

"I didn't even know I had a sister," said Emmazel, swallowing.

~

In the days that followed, Emmazel found herself swept up in a whirl of decorations and decisions, and she felt deeply out of her element. Kendra managed everything and made any decision that Emmazel found crippling, which kept things moving forward. Emmazel kept reminding herself that the party was officially as much for Kendra as for Mrs. E, to keep herself from feeling too upset at being sidelined.

"I still can't believe that my father hasn't yet realized that

I've been leaving my tower," she commented to Heather and Kendra one day as they were selecting music to play during the dancing. A few of Emmazel's companions had been musicians, but the instruments that the Flaxseeds' orchestra played were astonishing. "I'm gone for hours every day, and my garden is now outside, but he hasn't said a word." She frowned. "Maybe he just doesn't care."

"You did want his approval," said Heather, frowning.

"I did … but I think actually I wanted him to *care*." Emmazel ran her thumb down a page of sheet music. "I don't think he approves; I don't think he'll ever approve. I think he's given up the quarrel before even trying to argue."

"I'm sorry," said Kendra. There was an echo of a sympathetic smile that flashed in the corner of her eyes, though she was still *just* trying to be polite.

"He's getting old, though. Maybe he's just too tired to argue." Maybe Night had already advised him to leave her alone, and her father had agreed.

"So, what do you think of this piece?" Kendra prompted.

"I think it's good." Emmazel sighed and handed back the sheet of paper. "If you think it's best, then I have no objections."

Kendra nodded and added the page to the stack. "It's one of my favorites, and I thought you would like it, too."

"Oh? A favorite?" asked Emmazel. For all the decisions she made, Kendra rarely expressed a real preference. She did what she thought best and what she thought would be the most pleasing, but seldom what she *wanted*. It was almost terrifying.

"Yes. It was the piece they played when…" Kendra suddenly stiffened and looked up at the wall. "It doesn't matter. It's one of my favorites. That's all. I love how the song wraps around one's heart and makes one think of hopes, dreams, and love."

"I like that!" said Heather. "I completely agree! I never thought of that song this way before, but you're completely right. It's very charming."

And here she gave a massive sigh that betrayed the cheer of

her exclamation. She still had not recovered from her disappointment with Sir E. Emmazel held back a sigh of her own.

"It's beautiful," she agreed. "I fully understand why it's your favorite."

A smile worked at Kendra's lips, but she turned away. "We still have a few more pieces to select, though, with the guidance we have, I think we can safely leave the rest to the musician's judgment, so long as they keep in the spirit of our choices."

"Oh, yes, I do like that idea," said Emmazel, releasing a breath of relief. "It will give an element of surprise and mystery." And she wouldn't need to make any more choices based on music she didn't know.

"I'll give the instructions," said Kendra, and then silence hung heavy in the room before she continued. "Will you stay long enough for refreshment, or should you be returning already?"

"I can stay a while longer," said Emmazel. "If that's all right with you."

She and Heather should probably have been leaving, but she did not yet feel ready for the walk back home. It was a truly frightful journey!

"I will call for the refreshments," said Kendra.

"I really hope you don't consider us a bother," Emmazel continued on as they took seats on the couch, Emmazel and Heather beside each other and Kendra across from them. "You've done so much for us, and we're truly grateful. I couldn't have done any of this on my own."

Kendra's lips pinched. "My parents wanted to throw the party, and I needed the distraction. Thank you for coming to keep me company these last few weeks and keeping the focus off of myself."

"Then you're very welcome," said Emmazel. She leaned forward. "Would you tell me what's the matter? Perhaps sharing your troubles would make them seem lighter. And though I've lived in a tower my whole life, I'm … generally good at giving advice."

But Kendra just drew back, her eyes hardening. "I don't need my private affairs pried into," she said. "They're not your concerns, and there's no advice in the world that can help me. Let me plan this party for you, and that is enough for me."

"Very well." Emmazel took a deep breath and leaned back against the cushions. "I understand. Thank you."

But she *did* want to know what troubled Kendra. If only the girl trusted her more! She was sure she could do *something* to help!

A servant saved the awkward silence, not with the promised refreshments but with an announcement of visitors. Prince Earnest had returned, this time with his wife and family.

"Oh!" cried Kendra, leaping to her feet. "They're earlier than expected, but it is fortunate that they have arrived while Emmazel is here. Show them in and tell the cook to send enough for our new guests as well."

Emmazel ran the loop of her braid through her hands, her heart hammering into her throat. Mrs. E was here. Already. What was she going to do?

Just minutes later, the door swung open, and Sir E stepped through with a woman on his arm. The sheer wave of power surrounding her was overwhelming and sent Emmazel's mind spinning again. Beside her, Heather hastened to her feet and dipped into a curtsey.

"Your highness," she breathed.

But Mrs. E's gaze was fixed on Emmazel, and the world wavered around her.

An older woman stepped around Mrs. E, placed a bundle in her arms, and then rushed to Emmazel.

"It's you!" she cried. "You're all grown up, but it's you. Oh, Emmazalea, I've missed you – and here you are!"

Emmazel stood automatically and allowed the woman to wrap her in a hug. This, this felt right. Her sister, who she barely remembered but immediately recognized as the missing piece of her heart that she'd been unable to replace for so long.

"I see you're out of your tower still, Emmazel," said Sir E. "I didn't expect to find you here."

"Well, there's no reason for me to stay in my tower, is there?" said Emmazel, as she pulled away from her sister. "And since Kendra's come home and has needed a friend, here I am. After all, Berry has said for years that we were destined for friendship."

"I'm glad you have friends," said her sister.

"Father made sure I wasn't alone," Emmazel assured her, and she frowned. "I don't remember your name."

Her sister just smiled. "You were young when you left, and frankly, I've only just remembered my own name, myself. It's Foxglove."

"Foxglove, yes. Right." Emmazel nodded. "I suppose you would like to see father again. Since you've been gone so long."

"Oh, certainly," said Foxglove, squeezing Emmazel's shoulder. "But it grows late today, and I planned to make my visit tomorrow. But I'm so glad to see you now!"

"It was a surprise, yes," said Emmazel. "All of this. Especially..." Her gaze drifted back to Mrs. E and her husband. "Father never really told me anything, as Sir E might have said. So this has all been quite a shock."

"I found it shocking myself when the Forest abducted me, and I found out that it wanted me to take the place of its current Mistress," said Mrs. E, taking another step forward, and Emmazel finally properly looked at the woman.

She was *green*.

Well, not *entirely* green – her skin was a natural color slightly darker than Emmazel's own, and her hair was brown, but she had patches of green plant substance on her face and arms and an actual rose vine growing through her hair. And the bundle in her arms was a *baby*.

"I'm sorry that I was hiding in a tower and couldn't take the burden from you," said Emmazel stiffly.

Mrs. E gave a weak smile as Sir E guided her to a place on the sofa, then caught a young boy who was running about the room and sat down beside her.

"It's done," she said. "I'm just glad that the Mistress is gone. She truly was a villain." Her gaze flickered to Heather. "I take it that you're the young lady?"

"Yes," said Sir E, and they left it there in awkward silence. Emmazel frowned as she realized that there was more being said between them. The words weren't audible, but Emmazel could hear a whisper against her subconscious like the plants' song – though she couldn't *quite* make out what they said to each other.

The servants finally arrived with food, and small talk was made while they ate, driven mainly by Kendra and Foxglove. Introductions were made to make things less awkward, but Emmazel still didn't really care to learn any other names for the E's. She was still quite miffed that he had somehow been married *with children* the whole time she thought he was courting Heather.

She didn't catch the son's name, but the daughter, the daughter!

"We named her for you, actually," said Mrs. E. "Azalea. Elazalea, specifically, and only after her birth did the Forest point me in your direction. It didn't know where you were, but it had forgotten that this country lay in this direction, and now here we are. And here you are! Would you like to hold Ela?"

Emmazel drew back, staring at the baby. "I – are you sure? You barely know me. I've never held a baby before!"

"If you don't want to, it's fine. I just thought I would offer," said Mrs. E. "Because maybe we've only just met, but you're still family, and I hope that we can soon heal everything that the Mistress has broken."

Emmazel chewed her lip and then took another bite of her cupcake. She shook her head. "I think … I think that this is all just a little bit too much all at once."

Mrs. E nodded. "I understand. After all, you have lived in a tower for the last forty years."

Emmazel took a sharp breath as a number was finally given to her life. "You … know how long I've been in the tower?"

"I know how long it's been since your father took you away," Mrs. E explained. "Do you *not* know? Well, it's been forty-one years, more accurately. You were five years old when you left the Forest, but you might not remember it."

She leaned against her husband, and another inaudible whisper passed between them as she stared at her baby.

"I don't." Emmazel gripped her plate tighter, then set it down and stood. "Well, I do think that Heather and I should be returning home. Thank you for letting us visit, Kendra."

Heather frowned as she stood. "But…"

"It was good to see you again, Emmazalea," said Foxglove. "I will plan to visit the tower tomorrow, because I'm eager to see Father again. I'm glad we could find you again before it was too late."

"Yes," said Emmazel, and she pulled Heather out of the room.

## 16

Father was sitting in his armchair as Heather and Emmazel climbed through the window. Night sat on the back of the chair but hopped down and disappeared down the stairs before anyone could say anything. Heather gave Emmazel a fearful, not at all helpful glance, muttered something about fixing dinner, and then disappeared after him.

Emmazel and her Father stared at each other for a long minute, and excuses and arguments whirled through her head. She spoke none of them as long as he remained silent. So long as she had no idea what he really thought.

Finally, he gave a long sigh and shut his book. "Did you girls enjoy yourselves?"

Emmazel breathed in sharply and nodded. "We did. I'm sorry, I know you don't want me to leave the tower, but I just can't live in the tower anymore. I just *can't.*"

"I always knew that once you tasted freedom, you wouldn't be able to give it up," he said and then gave a long sigh. "I kept you safe while it mattered, and now there's nothing more for me to do."

"Oh, Father." Emmazel rushed forward to take his hand and throw herself on the ground at his side. "I'm sorry. I didn't mean to hurt you, but I *must* learn how to live in the world. You can't protect me forever."

"No, I can't." Father's shoulders sagged as he stared at her. "I had hoped, though…"

Emmazel patted his hand. "I'll be fine, Father. I promise." She took a deep breath. "Sir E returned today. He brought Mrs. E back with him. And her mother. Foxglove. She's coming tomorrow and looking forward to seeing you again."

Father looked up, and his shoulders lifted. "Foxglove. Yes. She'll take care of you. The dear girl – it will be good to see her again."

"Let's get you some dinner and then to bed." Emmazel patted his hand again and then stood. "And, please, don't worry about me."

He smiled up at her. "I'm afraid I'll always worry about you. I've been doing it too long to give it up now."

She gave a quiet laugh and kissed the top of his head. "I love you, Father."

"I hope the world treats you well, my dear," he answered. "It's good that you have family again to take care of you. I hope that you and Elinrose can work together."

Emmazel wrinkled her nose. "We shall see. The world has changed, and all I know for sure is that I have a lot to learn."

"Are you sure you don't want to stay in this tower?"

"Alas, I've already moved my garden outside, and it's too late." Emmazel shook her head. "Let me go see how Heather is coming with supper."

She took a deep breath as she walked down the stairs, trying to calm her fraying nerves. Yes, her father's acceptance was just as bad as any other reaction she had feared. Because she knew that he still didn't approve, and he likely never would. Her father wasn't perfect, but he'd sacrificed so much for her and her safety. She didn't like that this distance might mar her final days with him.

Heather had dinner well in hand, and Night watched her from a kitchen chair, his tail lashing back and forth. She glanced over her shoulder at Emmazel and offered a reassuring smile, though she seemed reluctant to *say* anything.

Emmazel gave a weak smile of her own, shrugged, and then

scooped Night up for a hug. If he was going to insist on acting like a normal cat around Heather, then she might as well treat him like one. He wasn't going to say anything to comfort her.

"Life used to be so simple," she confessed. "And now I fear I don't know anything."

"The more you learn, the more you find out you don't know," said Heather.

"So I'm discovering." Emmazel scratched Night behind his ears and buried her face in his fur. He tolerated this for a minute, then gave an overly cat-like yowl and clawed his way out of her arms. Emmazel let him go. She might punish him for his determination to act like a fool, but she wasn't going to torture him.

"You're doing well," Heather assured her. "I'm sure that soon no one would ever know that you grew up in a tower."

Emmazel nodded and rolled her eyes at Night, who was trying to groom his fur back into order. "Silly cat."

He gave her a glare and then bounded upstairs. They would likely argue about it later, but she felt better for now.

~

Emmazel felt even better the next morning, and she hurried through her morning routine so she could get outside as quickly as possible. She was going to see Foxglove again, and she couldn't wait to learn more about the sister she hadn't known she had.

How little she knew about her sister! Foxglove appeared much older than herself – and she had grown daughters and grandchildren. She'd had a whole life – all while Emmazel had lived in a tower.

No, no. She wouldn't let herself be jealous of her sister. Foxglove had suffered, too. She hadn't been hidden safely away. Now their mother was gone, and it all was over. They were able to heal.

"Emmazel! You're outside! What miracle is this?"

Emmazel turned away from her apricot tree to see Anna. Quickly, she put down her trowel and rushed to give her friend a hug. "I know! It's so strange, but here I am!"

"I told you that you would thrive out here and look at you!" Anna gave Emmazel a tight squeeze and then pulled back to smile at her.

Emmazel inclined her head. "I won't tell you that you were right," she said. "My father had good reasons to keep me in the tower. But I'm out of it now and glad for my freedom."

"Ah, yes, his reasons!" Anna shook her head and took a step back. "Well, you're free now, and what are you going to do with yourself? Oh, and you *must* tell me exactly how you convinced your father to let you out. And yourself, because I've always been convinced that you were really the one keeping yourself inside."

She wasn't wrong. "Once I made up my mind, there was nothing he could do, and I think he always knew that. I … found out *why* he kept me inside, and now it's up to me to decide what to make of it. I'm still deciding, but for now, I've moved my garden outside and am planning a party."

"Oh? A party!"

"I need to do something to improve my reputation. I can't keep being the witch of the tower if I'm no longer in my tower. Besides…" She trailed off as she saw her sister's approach. "Foxglove!"

Emmazel pushed past Anna and threw her arms around Foxglove's neck. Foxglove hugged her back immediately, holding her tight.

"And who's this? I've never seen you about Hightower, ma'am."

Anna hovered as Emmazel and Foxglove pulled apart, but her smile was friendly.

Foxglove just laughed. "Ah, well, this is the first time I've set foot in this country; most of my life has been spent in the Forest or on the other side of the mountains in the North Country," she explained. "I'm Emmazel's older sister, and you are?"

"My most recent companion before Heather," Emmazel quickly explained, as Anna drew back with raised eyebrows.

"She recently married a duke, and so she had to leave me, but she remains a dear friend just the same."

Foxglove nodded and then pulled Anna into a hug. "It's good to know that she's been taken care of. We've worried about her."

"And well you should have!" Anna declared. "Trapped in a tower the way she has been. Where have you been all this time? And her mother, too!"

"Our mother is why she had to be in the tower," Foxglove shook her head. "And for most of this time, I was a broken shell of myself with no memory of who I was. I'm not as strong a Sensitive as either Emmazel or Elinrose, and since Emmazel should have been our mother's heir, Mother would have killed her if she'd been able to find her."

Anna's eyes went wide. "Killed her? Her own mother!"

"Our mother wasn't a good woman," said Foxglove. "But now she's gone, and I've found where Father has hidden Emmazel all these years. I'm here now." She pinched her lips together as she stared up at the tower. "Is Father inside?"

"I think so," Emmazel glanced up at the tower. "He doesn't like to stay inside, but it's early, and I told him you were coming. He's looking forward to seeing you again."

"And you use the vines to come and go?" Foxglove took a step towards the tower, reaching out to them. "You really are strong, if you've been able to use them within the null space of the tower. Earnest says that it was so suppressive that he could barely take a step into the tower without feeling that he was being choked."

That was probably why he seldom left the windowsill when he visited. Emmazel realized that she probably should have questioned that. She should have questioned a *lot* about Sir E, but here she was.

The vines unwound at Foxglove's request, though they were even more sluggish than they were for Heather. Foxglove frowned and shook her head. "I don't think I'll ever really regain what Mother stole from me, and I was never strong."

"If you would like to go on ahead and speak to Father alone, you can," said Emmazel. "Just … be aware that he's … *old* now."

Foxglove gave a weak laugh. "Well, so am I."

She took hold of the vines, and Emmazel added a silent order of her own as she asked them to carry her to the window.

"You have a *sister!*" cried Anna as she disappeared inside.

"I *know!*" Emmazel shook her head. "I can scarcely believe it, either, I swear. But here she is, and her daughter, and that's why I'm throwing this party."

"And what was she saying about you being your mother's heir? What is that supposed to mean?"

"I don't really understand it, but I was apparently supposed to rule a Forest." She retreated to her garden and knelt before her roses. "But now it seems that Foxglove's daughter rules this Forest instead, and I don't know what to do."

Anna put a hand on Emmazel's shoulder. "Do you think she'll misuse the power?"

Emmazel tensed, and she buried her hands in mint leaves to steady her nerves. "I barely know anything about her, except that she's the Gardener instead of me."

"But surely you can't judge her just on that," said Anna. "Unless you think there was something sinister in the way she took the throne. But if your sister's correct, then your mother needed to be removed and it's what has given you your freedom."

"I know, but I can't help but keep asking myself why it had to be her and not me." Emmazel yanked a weed out of the soil and tossed it away – they were far more aggressive now that her pots were outside, but that was only to be expected. "I'm free now, but it's only to learn that I had a purpose, a *reason* to exist, and someone else took it before I had a chance to choose it."

"Ah." Anna nodded. "Well, dear Emmazel, if you want my advice – don't let this fester into resentment towards your family. Family is precious, and your freedom is a gift. You *will* find another purpose – I know you will."

"Maybe."

"You're free from your tower. You *will*. Keep an open mind, Emmazel. Maybe I should bring you to court with me."

Emmazel drew back, blinking. "Court? Oh, no – I'm still adjusting to Hightower. I really don't think I could handle more people than that."

"Perhaps not yet," said Anna. "But bear it in mind. I would love to introduce you to society – I'm sure you would dazzle them."

"The only people I'm hoping to dazzle right now are those attending my party next week," Emmazel answered. "Let me overcome *that* hurdle before I start thinking about courts."

"Very well, but you're going to do fine, I assure you."

Emmazel hoped she was right.

"Do you think you might be able to attend the party?" she asked. "It's only a week away, and I will need to ask Kendra to rearrange the guestlist, but it would mean the world to me to have you there."

"And I owe you the world for what you've done for me," said Anna. "I will make it happen; just tell me the date and where it will be."

"I think, if you're there, then I won't have anything to worry about."

"No, you won't, though you never had anything to worry about to begin with." Anna laughed. "I've told you, my friend, that you're a treasure to the world, and it will be glad to have you."

"We'll see," said Emmazel.

"Perhaps we should go see how your father and sister are doing," Anna suggested. "Because I want to know more about her, and I think you haven't asked as many questions as you should. I don't know if you've noticed her dress, but she's well off. Now, maybe this Gardener business means she's a princess of some sort, but I would like to make sure."

"I'll see if she and Father would like to come down," Emmazel countered. "I'd like to show her my garden."

## 17

Foxglove had been a *queen*.

True, she only had become queen after their mother had drained her power and left her in the barren North Country without her memory, but she had been a queen nonetheless.

It also meant that Mrs. E had been a princess, which was only natural, given that Sir E was a prince. Yet another way that she was Emmazel's superior.

Oh, she *claimed* that a princess was no different than any other girl, but the fact remained that she had been raised among the whirl of society and knew how to handle herself with grace and decorum no matter what.

Having grown up in a tower, where socialization had *entirely* different rules, Emmazel found it infuriating to watch. It was almost impossible to hate the woman, and it only made Emmazel feel all the more inferior.

But the week sped by, and Mrs. E was only ever kind, amiable, and steady. Meanwhile, Emmazel felt increasingly out of her element as she compared herself to the younger woman. Mrs. E was only twenty-nine and had already vanquished a villain, claimed a throne, married and had two children, and was a trusted advisor for not one but *four* neighboring kingdoms.

All while Emmazel lived in a tower and tricked a succession

of lords into marrying her commoner companions.

At least *most* of Emmazel's companions and their husbands were grateful for her intervention. No complaints had reached her, save for her mistake with Heather.

She swept all of her worries away as the day of the party arrived. It was as glorious a day as she could have ever hoped, with the Flaxseeds' ballroom packed full of people eager to meet the witch of the tower for themselves. Emmazel wore a beautiful green dress far finer than anything she'd ever owned before, and Kendra's own handmaid had done her long, golden hair in an intricate weave of braids and curls.

Yet, as she stood awkwardly in the receiving line, trying to make small talk with a constant stream of people who had come to gawk at her, her eye couldn't help but often stray to Mrs. E, drifting effortlessly through the crowd, chatting easily with everyone. She proved as much a draw as Emmazel herself. After all, a rose vine grew out of her head.

"Oh, look at you! You look positively radiant tonight! Why, one would never know that, just weeks ago, you never wished to leave your tower, no matter what anyone else might say!"

Emmazel's gaze snapped away from Mrs. E as Anna and Lord Westbrook were the next in line for her to greet.

"I'm so glad you're here," she breathed. "I never thought so many people could fit in a single room!"

"It's quite a sight, isn't it?" Anna let go of her husband's arm to pull Emmazel into a hug. "I will confess that most ballrooms are larger than this and better able to handle such a crowd. You're quite the draw, my dear!"

"Well, myself and the Gardener." Emmazel bit her lip as her gaze went to Mrs. E again. "She seems so much more at home here than I am."

"She does, does she? Well, you're still doing very well for your first social event – why, the first party I hosted as Lady Westbrook, I wanted to run from the room! A thousand things went wrong, and I don't know how I survived it." Anna gave Emmazel another squeeze and then stepped back. "The Flaxseeds are here to deal with all the problems for you, so all you have to do is stand here and smile."

"I wish I was back in my tower."

She didn't, not really. Tonight was an exciting rush that she would never forget and she had wanted for so long. But this was also a world out of her control, and she desperately craved the command she had in her tower.

"Oh, but if you were back in your tower, then you wouldn't be here to enjoy this lovely evening." Anna shook her head. "Keep your chin up, my friend – it will be over before you know it, and you'll only chide yourself for not enjoying every moment while it happened. Now, I think I've taken enough of your time, though I'll be sure to find you later. Greet your next guest, and I'll go see if I can have a word or three with your dear niece, who looks almost as lovely as you! Are those *real* roses in her hair?"

"They grow there," Emmazel confirmed.

"Truly! Ah, then she is a strange one, and I know you!" Anna shook her head. "Oh, and I took the liberty of inviting a guest of my own, though I haven't seen him yet. Kendra gave me permission, so it's all right, but I *have* wanted you to meet him for some time!"

And she pushed on without any further explanation, leaving Emmazel to greet more guests. So many people who knew about her, but she knew little about them.

"You're doing well tonight, for your first social event."

It was Mrs. E standing beside her now, looking as pleasant and interested as ever. Emmazel took a sharp breath.

"So I've been told."

Mrs. E laughed. "Oh, no one can tell how nervous you are, I promise! You're made for events like this. Give it a year, and I don't think anyone would ever guess that you lived in a tower for forty years."

Emmazel folded her hands behind her back. "And yet *you* can tell?"

Mrs. E's smile fell, and her gaze drifted across the room. "I have become increasingly aware of you as time has passed. I think it's because of the way my magic is entwined with yours.

You're a daughter of the Forest, and I'm the Gardener."

Emmazel frowned. This did *not* make her feel better about this woman.

"I sense nothing from you."

"I've spent the last five years with my senses open to the Forest, and I'm currently away from it," Mrs. E explained. "You're currently trying to adjust to the noise of the world after living your life in a tower that suppressed your power as a Sensitive. You're trying to process far more information than you're accustomed to, while I'm dealing with far less, so of course, I'm going to notice more than you will."

Emmazel pinched her lips together. "I don't … I'm not…"

"If you're willing to take a word of advice, don't push yourself past what you're comfortable doing trying to be what you *think* people expect of you." Mrs. E rubbed at the rose vine growing in her hair, which Emmazel was learning was a sign she was nervous. "You will learn and grow as you adjust to your new life, but if you push yourself too fast because you think that's what you have to do, you're just going to burn out and disappoint everyone, especially yourself."

Emmazel bristled, hating this woman's nosiness. "I don't have anything to prove. Least of all to you."

"No, you don't. Remember that." Mrs. E sighed. "I know you resent me, but believe me when I say that this isn't what I wanted. I had a different life planned for myself, and I fought the Forest's call with everything I had. But here I am, and here you are, and we're both going to have to make the best of the situation. Austere put me where I needed to be, and I know He has a plan in all of this."

"I'm glad you know that." Emmazel hid a balled fist in her skirts.

Mrs. E's eyes darkened. "I've never discovered otherwise. Now, as wonderful as this party is, and I am grateful for the gesture, I am going to excuse myself for the night. I exhaust quickly when I'm away from the Forest, and Ela and Hansel aren't used to having me gone for long."

And she slipped away before Emmazel could protest, but

that didn't matter because, at that moment, the whole room erupted with a murmur of excitement as a new guest arrived.

~

Prince Christian was every inch as charming and dazzling as rumors claimed, and heat rushed to Emmazel's cheeks as he stood before her.

"Well, you must be the young woman I've heard so much about for all these years," he declared as his gaze swept her up and down. "And here I always thought I would have to climb a tower if I ever wanted to meet you for myself."

"Ah, well, I'm sorry to disappoint," said Emmazel, glancing down. "But my tower still stands if you should like to visit me there later." She winced as she realized how bad that sounded, but it was said now. "Me and my household, that is."

"Ah, yes, your household – of course." Christian gave her a roguish wink, and then he glanced out at the room. "I will be sure to visit, while I'm in the area. You have haunted my imagination for so many years now; indeed, I don't remember a time when tales of you weren't whispered by every gossip."

"I've been building my reputation for a while," she agreed. "Though I never truly thought that I would attract *you*, good prince."

"And yet here I am." Christian leaned forward. "Now, tell me. Have you had a chance to properly enjoy this party of yours, or have you stood here the whole night and only watched? Because, either way, there is some excellent dancing out there, and I insist on the privilege of standing with you at least once, if not twice, before the night is over."

"I would be honored," said Emmazel. "Though I must confess that I have never learned to dance, and that is why I'm standing here, watching."

"Ah, a pity." Christian shook his head. "I suppose there's no need for dancing in a tower – but since you are free tonight, you have *every* reason to enjoy yourself, and attending a party without dancing is a shame. Come along."

Emmazel's breath caught as he took her hand and pulled

her out to the floor. The music had just ended, and a new piece began. She recognized it as the one that Kendra had declared her favorite.

"Ah, this is a good one," he declared. "Easy to learn, so it's perfect for you. Now just relax, follow my lead, and let the music guide you."

It was hard to relax with her hand in his, but Emmazel tried her best. She always *had* wanted to dance, and having her first dance with Prince Christian was a glorious turn of events worthy of even her most wild imagination. That he didn't say a word about how clumsy her steps were or how often she trod on his foot made it so much better. Oh, but he was a true gentleman!

"It is a shame that I missed the guest of honor tonight – the *other* guest of honor, that is," Christian commented. "You were, of course, all the reason I needed to attend, but she sounds like quite the curiosity."

"Alas, Mrs. E grew tired and had to retire early," Emmazel said.

"Mrs. *E*, eh?" Christian repeated. "That's not quite the name that reached me."

"It's what *I* call her," Emmazel explained. "She's my niece, so it's my right to give her a nickname."

"Ah, of course." He laughed. "By all means, avail yourself of such a right. Still, it's so strange to think that we have neighbors we never knew about. I will make sure to speak to Prince Earnest before the night is over – who knows what alliances this could bring us."

"I hope it goes well for you," she answered. "I'm afraid that I know little of politics, even for as many of my former companions who married nobility."

"And one as pretty as yourself has no need for politics!" he assured her. "It would be a much better world without them, if you ask me. I know my life would be so much better if I didn't have my every move questioned and torn to shreds. Even my visit here will have a thousand repercussions, but I had our neighbor to meet, so I think I can get away with it."

"Why wouldn't you?" asked Emmazel.

"Because the Flaxseeds are not entirely in support of my family's rule." Christian gave a careless shrug. "And it's entirely reasonable, given the mess of sucession when my grandfather took the throne. Are you really unaware of this?"

"I'm not a fan of history," she confessed. "It seems hardly relevant when one lives in a tower, cut off from the rest of the world. I probably should care now that I've left my tower, though."

"It's a story and hardly a fitting conversation for such a setting," said Christian. "I shall have to make that visit to your tower to tell it to you. Ah!" And here the dance ended, so he guided her off of the floor. "Miss Kendra Flaxseed is looking especially pale tonight, have you noticed? My, but I've never seen a more unassuming young woman."

"She does like to fade into the background," Emmazel agreed, glancing Kendra's way. She felt a prickle of annoyance that the conversation had turned away from herself. "She was a lady's companion but recently returned home. It was quite unexpected, and I really thought that she was determined to climb through the court however possible. And, yet, here she is, and she won't tell me a word about what happened. I know something is bothering her, but she won't tell me what it is."

"Ever a private person is Kendra Flaxseed." Christian shook his head. "Ah, but it's hardly right to just sit here, talking about her behind her back. Do you think I should go introduce myself to her and see how she responds? Her parents won't like that, you know, but neither would they like me to snub her at her own party. I think I should go introduce myself. But don't worry, I'll be back for our second dance."

And with a grin and a wink, Christian left her side and melted into the party.

**18** Emmazel was still abuzz with nerves when she woke the next morning. She'd barely slept a wink after arriving home late, and now she bustled around the kitchen, preparing breakfast because Heather wasn't to be seen.

It was only now that she realized that she'd lost track of her friend during the party last night. With as many people as were in the room, she could hardly have been expected to always keep her eye on Heather. That she hadn't returned to the tower yet was disconcerting, but she probably had found somewhere else to stay the night.

Emmazel *hoped* that Heather had found somewhere else to stay the night.

She pulled together a breakfast of fruit and cream, left enough for her father, and then headed up the stairs to eat it in her sitting room. Just in case Heather returned while she ate, or she had some other visitor.

Night was absent, too, but that was hardly unusual. The black cat might call the tower his home, but he wasn't there all of the time. Only when he wanted to be fed or to snark at Emmazel. He really was an infuriating cat.

She paced about the room as she ate her breakfast. Her thoughts alternated between worrying over Heather and reminiscing every moment of the night before. Her first party.

She'd survived it. People had seen her as more than just the girl who lived in a tower, and she'd danced with the prince.

Not even Mrs. E's presence had been enough to truly dampen her enjoyment. It had been a glorious night.

Where was Heather?

Her fruit finished, she went to the window and stared outside. She wasn't *quite* ready to descend again – it was good to feel safe and secure in her fortress after the turmoil of the night before. Especially when she didn't know where to start a search for her friend.

Heather would come home on her own. She knew the village and countryside, and Emmazel didn't. Emmazel would just get herself lost if she was to go after her.

She should go tend her garden while she waited. It was pointless to sit here, worrying.

But, just to be safe, she took her bowl back down to the kitchen, first.

"Emmazel! Emmazel, come quick! I have an injured maiden here who claims to be your companion!"

She rushed back to the window. At the foot of the tower was Prince Christian, with Heather in his arms. Emmazel hurried down the vines as fast as they would lower her.

"What happened?" she demanded as she stepped onto the ground. "Will she be all right?"

"Emmazel!" cried Heather.

"I found her this morning on my morning walk," Christian explained. "She apparently got lost last night and turned her ankle in a hole. I'm glad I came along!"

"So am I!" Emmazel awkwardly shifted her weight from one foot to the other as panic and indecision rushed through her.

"How do we get her into the tower?" asked Christian. "I can't stand out here with her forever, after all."

"Oh! Right!" Emmazel raised a hand to command her vines. "Bring her here, and I'll take her right up."

Christian stepped forward, and his eyes went wide as the vines reached out to wrap around Heather and take her up to the window.

"I've heard the rumors that you command plants themselves, but I never quite believed them," he confessed. "You are a wonder, Emmazel."

Emmazel blushed under the praise and took hold of the vines herself to ascend into the tower. "I'll send vines down for you if you should like to follow."

A loud *mrowl* informed her that a particular cat had also returned home, so she offered Night a smile. "And one for you, too, Night."

And she hastened on before Christian could get *too* good a look at the color of her cheeks.

Heather had made it to an armchair and had collapsed into it, massaging her ankle. Her head shot up as Emmazel entered. "Oh, I'm so sorry!" she cried in a breathless rush. "I know I shouldn't have run away last night, and it was for the silliest reason, too, and now look at all the trouble I have caused!"

"Hush," Emmazel chided, kneeling before Heather to feel her ankle herself. It didn't seem to be broken, and that was good. "You're back here now, safe and sound, and that's all that matters." She pressed her lips into a line. "What *did* happen last night, though? I'm afraid I didn't notice your absence until this morning, but I've been worrying about you!"

Night appeared in the window and perched there, his tail wrapped around himself. "Prince Christian will come by later to ensure that she is well but doesn't want to intrude right now."

And then he hopped down and dashed up the stairs, leaving Emmazel agape and blinking.

~

"Did *you* know that the cat can talk?" Heather leaned in to whisper breathlessly in Emmazel's ear.

"Oh, Night never shuts up," Emmazel answered. She snapped her attention back to Heather and forced a shrug. "I don't know why he has taken so long to decide to let you know, but I try to respect his privacy. It's a dangerous world for talking cats."

"I imagine so." Heather took a long, pensive breath and then flopped back against the chair. "I was *such* a fool last night. Oh, Emmazel, I can't believe I was such a fool!"

"Well, people get hurt outside," said Emmazel. "It's why my father would much prefer that I stay in my tower at all times. Well, one reason why. Where did you go last night and why? And how did you hurt your ankle?"

Heather squeezed her eyes shut and shook her head. "I thought it would be fine to attend a party with him, and it was, at first. And he was so kind and polite, even offering to dance with me if I wanted to, but I just couldn't! The shame of it, Emmazel! Just looking at him, all I could think of was how silly I had been to think that he could possibly be there to court me, and I somehow thought that everyone could tell how silly I'd been, just by looking at me, and I couldn't bear to be in the room a moment longer. I *ran,* Emmazel. I ran from the room and into the night, got lost on my way back to the tower, stepped in a hole, and twisted my ankle."

"Oh, you poor thing." Emmazel reached over and patted Heather's hand. "I shouldn't have put you in that position – it was pure thoughtlessness of me! And to think of you alone and injured all night! It's a wonder that nothing worse happened to you."

"Well, it was frightening," Heather agreed, and her cheeks flushed. "But then Night found me. He couldn't help me out of the hole, but he stayed with me the whole night to keep me company. It was so strange to hear him speak – I thought I *had* to be imagining it, but I wasn't. I've always known that Night was a special cat, but now! How have I not seen it before?"

"He's a frustrating cat who was determined to keep you in the dark," Emmazel explained. "And, no, I don't know *how* he came to be able to talk. He can't tell anyone how it happened, or he'll lose the ability. Annoying as he can be, and no matter how much my curiosity burns, I can't find it in me to do such a thing to him. So, don't go asking him questions. It just upsets him."

Heather nodded solemnly. "I won't, then."

"Oh, but it shall be good to no longer have to pretend that he's a normal cat around you – you have no idea what a trial it is. It's my least favorite part of getting new companions, and, much as I understand why he doesn't speak to them until he trusts them, it's really quite infuriating when I want to talk to him but can't."

Heather nodded solemnly. "I can only imagine."

"But now, things will be so much nicer if everyone is talking to one another," Emmazel continued. "I don't know why he was so especially silly about not talking to you. Because he was." She shook her head. "I'm glad he was there for you. And that Prince Christian came along this morning to bring you home."

Heather sat up straight, then winced as she brushed her foot against the floor. "That was Prince Christian? I – I didn't realize! Oh, Emmazel, *Prince Christian* saved me and brought me home. What am I do to?"

"Thank him for his service when he returns to make sure you're okay." Emmazel shook her head as she stood to fetch some cream to put on Heather's ankle. "You were a damsel in distress, and our prince is a gentleman, of course he was going to rescue you."

"Last night was just one embarrassment after another," Heather muttered as she fell back again. "I think I shall always shudder to think on it, except—"

"Except what?" Emmazel tilted her head to the side as she found the jar she sought and some bandages, so she returned to Heather's side to apply the ointment and wrap her ankle.

"Emmazel," Heather dropped her voice to a whisper and leaned in again. "I think I've fallen in love again."

Emmazel sat up straight, pulling the bandage tight. "Have you?"

"Oh, I really think I have," Heather affirmed. "I know it seems impossible, and I admit that I might be the greatest fool of all to even consider him, but after what he's done for me, I cannot help it! I fear I have a heart that will never know sense."

Emmazel drew back, pressing her lips together as she considered. Heather and Christian! She'd never imagined such a thing, but why not? Heather deserved to be a princess, and *Sir E* was already married. And while Emmazel had flattered herself with thoughts of letting him win her own hand, this would be so much better all around.

However she might fantasize, however people said that she had been a natural last night, however she had enjoyed being the center of attention, Emmazel knew that the glitz and intrigue of court was not for her. No, if Heather's heart was set on Christian, then Christian she would have.

Emmazel smiled and finished tying the bandage. "It's never foolish to fall in love, and you're worthy of any young man you set your heart on. And after what he's done for you!"

"You … don't think I'm silly?"

"No, not at all." Emmazel shook her head and then stood. "Now, I'm going to go get breakfast for you, and you're going to stay right there. Sprained ankles are dreadful things, and you need to heal. I hope it goes well for you this time – but remember, not a word about him should pass between us. I don't need to hear his name, and we shouldn't even discuss this again. You can decide your heart for yourself, and oh! I'm glad to hear that you're moving on and loving again!"

Heather smiled back. "Oh, I'm so glad you approve. He really is wonderful."

*19* Christian came again that afternoon, but, unfortunately, Heather had already gone to her room for a nap. Emmazel couldn't bring herself to wake her and bring her back up the stairs with her ankle, so she resigned herself to entertain him on her own.

But, given that she needed to be more careful with *this* potential prince suitor than she had been with the last, it was a sacrifice she had to make. After risking Heather's heart once, she couldn't bear to do so again.

"So, this is your tower." Christian folded his arms over his chest as he stalked about the room and examined every inch of it. "Somehow, I always imagined there would be more signs of boredom. No endless knitting projects everywhere? No paintings covering every inch of the walls?"

"I'm not really an artist," Emmazel answered. "Most of my knitting projects get sold or given away to those in need, and it's really my garden that arrests most of my attention. It used to be upstairs, but I moved it outside when I left the tower.

"Ah!" Christian threw himself into a chair and leaned forward to stare at Emmazel. "You have quite the sanctuary here. I can see why you've never left it until now."

Emmazel gave a thin smile, inclining her head.

"So, how is the fair maiden I rescued this morning? Shall she recover, or is she injured for life?"

Oh, good, his first thoughts *were* for Heather! How

excellent!

"I think she shall recover," Emmazel answered. "I'm no doctor, but I know a few things about healing, and her injury doesn't seem too severe. She spent an entire night outside, so she's sleeping right now. Poor thing."

"Every time I think of her, alone last night, it's enough to make a man shudder." Christian leaned back and shook his head. "And if I hadn't come by when I did!"

"I would have let my father know, organized some form of search party, if much longer had passed," Emmazel assured him. "But it's so much better that you found her! Every second she was alone was a tragedy!"

"I find myself quite in agreement," said Christian. "But it is over now, and she shall recover. I must insist on seeing her again before I leave, though not yet, for she deserves her rest. In the meantime, I promised you proper conversation last night, and a gentleman never forgets his promises!"

"You need not feel so obligated!" Emmazel laughed.

"What is a prince without obligations?" Christian shook his head, all serious. "No, I am here for you to ask your questions, and I shall ask mine, and if we're not tired of one another by the end of it, then we shall get along famously!"

"I see!" Emmazel leaned back in her chair, fidgeting with the end of her braid. "Well, I'm in the habit of letting my visitors satisfy their curiosity first, for mine is oddly cool, by habit, and I'm also vain enough to enjoy talking about myself."

Christian tilted back his head to laugh. "Ah, such honesty! It's frankly refreshing after all the misdirection, false humility, and deception of court!"

Emmazel inclined her head. "It sounds frightful."

"Oh, it certainly is – and I consider you quite wise for hiding away from such things in this tower." Christian shifted forward again. "So, my questions about you. I've already seen for myself that you're just as beautiful and enchanting as the rumors claim, and it baffles me even more that it's always your companions that my noblemen marry – though they've all been charming women, to be certain."

"Until recently, I couldn't leave my tower," Emmazel pointed out. "No matter how attractive I might be, no man wants a wife he can't take home!" She shook her head. "It just wouldn't make sense."

"I suppose it would not," said Christian. "But now that you have left the tower, how will that change things?"

Emmazel opened and shut her mouth, then leaned back with a shrug. "I'm still not in a rush to begin a relationship. After all, I know so little about the world. I want to explore and learn who I am, first."

Christian's eyebrow arched.

"I'm not against the idea of it happening," she quickly explained. "If the right man came along, I wouldn't turn him away, but it's not what I want."

"I see." Christian nodded. "Well, I suppose you have time enough to wait with youth such as yours."

"I do, at that." Emmazel sat up straighter and decided that she would much prefer to *not* have him ask questions about herself. "So, have you met Kendra Flaxseed before? You seemed to recognize her last night, though she was only in court as a lady's companion."

"And you think I wouldn't take note of a mere companion?" he asked. "It's my business to know all of the pretty young women in court, regardless of their status. With that dour frown of hers, she barely qualifies for the position, but she's a Flaxseed, besides. Her family has stayed away from court for the last fifty years, so when she appeared, it was worth taking note."

"You said that they don't like your parents' reign?"

"Ah, yes, I promised you that story, didn't I?" Christian leaned back and shook his head. "It's not that exciting, but a promise is a promise."

~

"Fifty-five years ago, King Rand died without an obvious heir," Christian explained. "His wife had only given him a daughter, and Howsill doesn't allow daughters to inherit. The throne might have gone to her husband, but he had been lost to the Forest just a few weeks before King Rand's death. And, so, after long debate, it was decided to give the throne to my grandfather. He was the princess's cousin, but as the queen's nephew, not the king's. He had no royal blood, but he was an intelligent, just man, and most agreed that he would serve the country well as king. There was dissent, but none could suggest a better option, and so they moved forward, planning the coronation."

"Were the Flaxseeds among the dissent?" asked Emmazel.

"One of the most vocal," Christian confirmed. "They were far more powerful in court, back then, but even they could do nothing – until the princess bore a son just a week before the coronation."

"Oh!" Emmazel clapped her hands together. "And he *would* have a claim to the throne, wouldn't he?"

"Yes, but he was an infant, and everything had been arranged," Christian countered. "Howsill had already been without a king for six months, and the princess didn't wish to place the crown on her son's head when he was just a baby. Accusations were thrown. Both sides claimed the other only wanted power, but in the end, my grandfather was crowned, as had been planned, with the princess's full support, and every noble who argued otherwise was banished from court until he could establish his reign."

"What became of the little prince, then?" asked Emmazel.

"Oh, yes. He inherited his father's title and lives quietly away from court, most of the time," Christian explained. "Westbrook sometimes jests that he'll have to take the crown from me if I should prove too irresponsible to properly appreciate it, but I know he would never want it for himself."

"Westbrook!" Emmazel repeated, sitting up straight.

"Yes, Westbrook," Christian repeated, standing. "If things had been different, he would have been king. He doesn't make use of his royal blood, and many have forgotten, but he would have been a good king in that other life."

"I'm sure he would have been," said Emmazel, easing back

into a smile. "He seemed a good man, when he was visiting. I wouldn't have let Anna marry him otherwise, after all. But, to think that he was royalty!"

"I know – he's the most unassuming gentleman in the world." Christian shook his head. "Well, I don't know how much longer I can stay – I do have duties to my country, after all, since my cousin has left me to it. I hope you have a lovely rest of your day, Miss Emmazel, and that you someday find the fullest love that you deserve."

"Thank you." Emmazel laughed politely. "I hope the same for you."

"Ah, but I'm a prince." Christian shook his head. "I'll marry for political reasons – unless a miracle should happen." He laughed. "Do you think I might see the invalid before I go? Having been the one to save her, I feel responsible for her recovery, and I know not when I shall return."

"Of course," said Emmazel, quickly standing. "I'll go see how she is and if she would like to see you."

Yes, this was very good. No love potions were even needed. Prince Christian would have his miracle, and he and Heather would be happy, indeed!

20 Life quieted now that the ball was over, and Emmazel sought a new routine. Prince Christian had returned to his royal life, and Emmazel tried to not fret at his absence. It would be easier if she knew when he would return. How was he to build a relationship with Heather if he was gone? How was Emmazel supposed to work her miracle?

She threw herself into her gardening to avoid her troubled thoughts. Her plants were thriving in the sunlight, and the potions she had made in the last few weeks had worked better than ever. Emmazel had even been able to sell her potions herself at market, though Heather still handled the bartering and money. Emmazel just didn't understand money.

She would have to learn, though. So she could be ready once Christian returned to woo Heather. It was only a matter of time.

Who *hadn't* left yet? Sir E and his wife, of course. They and their children still stayed with the Flaxseeds. And so did Foxglove.

Emmazel was happy enough to have her sister nearby. It almost made up for the presence of the rest. She and Heather visited the Flaxseeds once a week, where they continued their awkward friendship. It was far nicer when Foxglove visited the tower. Mrs. E visited as well, which was less nice, but Sir E thankfully stayed away.

She wasn't sure what she would have done if *he* should return to her tower. The horrid man.

"So, what will you be doing today?" she asked Heather over breakfast. "I don't have anything for you to do, so you're quite at your own leisure."

Heather's eyes lit as she stabbed her eggs. "Oh! I was thinking of taking Night to explore the woods," she declared. "So I can get to know them better and not get lost again."

"That sounds like a wonderful idea to me," said Night, not looking up from his own plate of eggs.

Emmazel frowned. Heather's ankle had healed – that wasn't the problem. Truly, Emmazel didn't know how to put into words what bothered her. Now that Night was speaking to Heather, the two spent an inordinate amount of time together. Emmazel *wasn't* jealous about it. Merely … confused.

Night had never raised such a fuss over any of Emmazel's previous companions. He had never been so silly about speaking to one. He had *certainly* never spent so much time with one once he did speak to her.

But when had that cat *ever* made sense? Emmazel knew he could make friends however he liked. It was just…

As the rest of her life had spiraled out of control, Night had been a rock of normalcy for her to cling to – even as they had argued. Now he was slipping away, too. What had happened to his declarations of friendship?

No, no, banish that thought. Night knew what Heather meant to Emmazel; that was all. And Heather needed to be distracted from Christian's absence. Emmazel wouldn't sink into petty resentment just because her two dear friends got along so well.

"I'll garden," she finally said awkwardly. "Like always."

"Oh," said Heather, with a frown of her own. "You could join us, too, if you'd like. I don't want you to feel left out, and you should probably learn the woods, too. So you won't get lost in them, either."

Emmazel forced herself into a smile. "Oh, but you know

how I love my garden! No, you and Night enjoy yourselves and don't worry about me."

Heather's face lit again. "We will! Enjoy ourselves, that is! Thank you!"

Emmazel's smile turned brittle, but she held it in place by sheer force of will.

Night finished his eggs and leapt down from the table to wrap around Emmazel's legs. "It won't be the same without you, dear Emma. But I completely understand that you don't want to drag your braid through the leaves and dirt. Think of how terrible it will be to clean it!"

Emmazel pushed him away with her foot. "Keep such opinions to yourself, you troublesome cat."

"And here I thought for a moment that you might miss me!"

"I can't believe that I ever resented your silence! Oh, that you had never deigned to talk to Heather!"

Heather's eyes widened, and she darted around the table to scratch a disgruntled Night behind his ears. "*I* don't resent your ability to speak," she told him, in an exaggerated whisper, holding pointed eye contact with Emmazel. "I think she's just tired. So let's leave her to her garden – because you know she's always in so much a better mood after she's spent a few hours with her plants."

"A very good point," said Night.

~

And so Emmazel was left behind in her garden while her two companions explored the woods without her. She shouldn't have let them shut her out like that, but what could she have done? She *wasn't* jealous, and that's exactly how it would have appeared if she had pushed herself between them.

"Ah! Hello, Emmazel! I was hoping that you would be home today."

Emmazel spun around and stiffened as she saw Mrs. E approaching. Oh, she really *should* have gone with Heather and Night!

"Hello," she answered and then narrowed her eyes as a small, black puppy rushed ahead of Mrs. E and darted in circles around Emmazel, yapping at her.

"Oh! Hansel! Leave her alone!" cried Mrs. E, rushing forward to grab the puppy by the scruff of his neck. He darted out of her grasp and continued to bark. Mrs. E gave Emmazel a long-suffering glance and thrust her baby into Emmazel's arms.

Emmazel stood awkwardly, not sure what to do with the baby. Ela was asleep, thankfully, but she could wake at any moment, and what would Emmazel do then?

Mrs. E caught the puppy, thankfully, and hugged it close, whispering in its ear. A moment later, the creature melted into the form of her son. She looked up and met Emmazel's eye apologetically.

"It's something he started doing yesterday," she explained. "He can control it – thankfully! – but Earnest and I don't know if it's from him or me. Is it leftover transformation magic, or is this what a son of the Forest can do? I know there hasn't been a son of the Forest in generations, but male sensitives tend towards an affinity towards animals, the way we can talk to plants. The way that Frosts and Zephyrs or Cinders and Dwarven have the same magic, but it presents differently depending if it's a man or woman. Perhaps it's both?"

"I didn't even know we were *called* Sensitives until you used the term." Emmazel gave a helpless shrug. "Didn't know I was a daughter of the Forest until your husband told me."

When was Mrs. E going to take Ela back?

But Mrs. E just shifted Hansel to her shoulder and rubbed his back. "I'm sorry – the whole matter has been a terrible mess from beginning to end, and your mother left so many broken lives in her wake."

"So I'm told."

Mrs. E frowned. "I was hoping your father would be here so I could ask him about Hansel. I doubt he'll know anything more than I do, but until I can return to the Forest…"

"And why don't you just return?" Emmazel shifted her grip

on Ela. If she was going to be stuck with the baby, she could at least hold her more comfortably.

Mrs. E's eyes flashed as she met Emmazel's gaze. "Because, right now, you're more important. Things are uneasy between us because of your mother's choices, and we need to determine what sort of relationship we are to have. Right now, you're antagonistic towards me, and I certainly can't leave as long as that's the case."

"You see me as a threat?" Emmazel raised her eyebrow, feeling satisfied that she could gain such a response from the woman.

"Potentially, yes," Mrs. E answered. "I don't want you to be one; I want you to be an ally for me to rely on. But I don't fear you. You're strong, yes, but you're scared of yourself and aren't fighting *for* anything. You want safety and security. You won't risk everything for an unknown. And the Forest, to you, is an unknown."

"I—" Emmazel swallowed. "I don't…"

"But, if we were friends, we don't have to worry about that," Mrs. E continued. "You'll be safe, and you can have a home."

"I can't help but feel that you're threatening," Emmazel said.

"It's not what I want. I don't want to fight." Mrs. E rubbed her forehead. "Is your father home?"

Emmazel shook her head. "He's often away, unless he's sleeping. I don't know where he goes. I've never asked. It's never mattered to me."

Mrs. E nodded. "Well, then. Do you mind if I stay and we visit until he returns? It would be a wonderful chance for us to work on our relationship."

"You're devious, you know that?" Emmazel sighed. All she would have to do to avoid Mrs. retreat was retreat into her tower, for the woman had never stepped foot in it.

But Emmazel didn't want to return inside. It was bad enough that she had let Night and Heather go off without her. Cutting herself off from the world would suffocate her.

"And you are distrustful." Mrs. E lowered Hansel to the ground and *finally* took Ela back from Emmazel. "You distrust yourself most of all."

Emmazel opened and shut her mouth, not sure how to answer that.

Mrs. E turned away, and Emmazel heard her give a nearby bush a silent order, and the bush wove itself into a cradle. Mrs. E laid Ela into the cradle and then sat down on the grass.

Emmazel bristled at her niece clearly showing off, but she wasn't going to rise to it. Instead, she turned away and knelt beside her cucumber vine. "Well, if I don't trust myself, how can I trust anyone else?"

"Exactly," said Mrs. E.

Emmazel frowned. She'd been trying to make a *point*, not have that woman *agree* with her!

"You know, the Forest is almost a prison, for me, as the Gardener," Mrs. E continued. "This is only the second time I've been able to leave it since it claimed me, and I want to savor it, even without needing to work on our friendship. The North Country, where I grew up, was completely cut off by the Forest, and while I'm happy that I am able to facilitate travel again for others, as the Gardener, I can't help but feel wistful that I don't get to experience the world I've saved."

Oh, yes, Mrs. E *would* see herself that way – the self-sacrificing savior of the world. Emmazel rolled her eyes without thinking. "How tragic for you."

"Not nearly as tragic as living your whole life in a tower, I quite agree," said Mrs. E. "We should make the most of it since we're both free. I know you have all the time in the world, but I don't, and I want to see as much of Howsill as I can while I'm here. Perhaps forge some alliances?"

"Don't let me stop you." Emmazel moved on to tend her lavender.

"Earnest and I are planning a trip to Boxill, the capital," Mrs. E continued. "You can come with us if you would like. In fact, I rather wish you would. You would do well to push your limits now that you've gained your freedom."

Emmazel chewed her lip and took a deep breath. She couldn't say no. Mrs. E would just accuse her of being too scared to test her limits. And she wasn't scared. She *wasn't*.

Okay. She was.

That wasn't a bad thing, was it? Emmazel had lived her whole life in a tower. What could anyone expect of her?

But had she really left her tower if she stayed at its foot? If she only strayed to the nearby village and no further? Was she really free if she couldn't escape her own fear?

Mrs. E didn't see her as a threat because she was too fearful to fight for anything. Maybe it was time to prove her wrong.

"That sounds lovely," Emmazel finally said. "I'm sure Heather will love it."

Mrs. E's lips curled into a smile, and Emmazel was sure that she'd heard her turmoil of thoughts as surely as if she had spoken them aloud. That's just how annoying she was.

"I'm sure she will – I look forward to the outing," she said. "You know, if you'd been there, in the Forest, five years ago, I would have happily let you face the Mistress in my place, if you had shown even the slightest interest. And even now, if I could step aside and part from the Forest without risking my very life, I would – provided I felt it would be safe with you. But you weren't there, and now I can't walk away."

"It's not my fault that I wasn't there."

"I know. Neither was it mine."

*21* Mrs. E left. Eventually. Heather and Night returned to the tower. Eventually. Emmazel's nerves remained frayed.

Why couldn't that woman just go away and stay away, instead of forcing herself where she wasn't wanted?

Emmazel paced her apothecary – it was so empty without her plants filling every inch of it, but she still made potions here. She needed to make more for her next trip to market tomorrow, but just couldn't find it in herself to focus on the ingredients.

Deep breaths. She could do this. She did these potions in her *sleep*.

"Is this you, hard at work? My, Emmazel, maybe your father is right, and you really should have never left the tower."

Emmazel's eyes flashed as she spun around to face Night. "Oh! You! Why must you always act like this? You're annoying, you know that?"

"And you take too much to heart right now," Night answered. "Why don't you sit down and take a deep breath? I'm sure things can't be as bad as you think. I mean, they could be, but you have a terrible habit of letting your imagination run away with you, and it distorts things far out of proportion,"

Emmazel glared at him for a moment more, then turned away and kept pacing. "I wish Sir E had never stepped foot in

Howsill," she said. "I wish he had stayed away and never even heard of my tower."

"I quite agree with you," said Night. "I did my best to scare him off before he could get to you, and I tried to warn you against him, but both were a fruitless endeavor, and there's nothing we can do now. I think he would have brought his wife here regardless of our actions, just because he knew you were here."

Emmazel paused and turned to him, hands on her hips. "You're not going to lecture me over the fact that she's my family and I need to accept her?"

"Perhaps you should," said Night. "She is your family. But I learned long ago to take no gifts from her kind, and I do not like that she is here, meddling." He added, in undertone, "I don't like remembering where you came from."

"I can't do anything about that." Emmazel gave a quiet huff.

"No, you can't. Neither can your father, no matter how much he wants to wish your mother away," Night answered, raising his chin. "She might be dead now, but her deeds remain."

Emmazel twisted away and threw up her hands. "What can I possibly do about that? I'm not responsible for anything that happened before I was born. And I've been trapped in a tower almost ever since."

"You have been," Night agreed. "But you are responsible for your own actions. Be careful, Emmazalea. Be very, *very* careful." His tail lashed back and forth. "I may not trust the Gardener myself, but I do admit that she is not the Mistress, and she can be a good influence on you."

Emmazel chewed her lip. "She's my *niece*. She should look up to *me*, not the other way around."

"Not being the most important person in a room is good for you, Emmazel," Night answered. "And if you chafe too hard, you can always sit in your tower window and shout down at her. Wouldn't that be a sight?"

Emmazel rolled her eyes before she picked him up by the

scruff of his neck, tossed him out of the room, and returned to her potions.

She still had several to make before morning, and she had been distracted for long enough.

~

"Well, isn't this a lovely sight – good to see you away from your tower again."

Emmazel gasped as she looked up to see Prince Christian leaning against her table. She glanced sidewise at Heather – who was haggling over the price of a cough syrup – and then lit into a smile. "Your highness! It's good to see you again! What brings you here of all places?"

Christian laughed, his grin as bright as ever. "To see you, of course! I stopped by your tower first, of course, but you weren't there. And then I remembered that your income comes from selling potions at market, and I wondered if you might be here. I'm so glad you are, for my next option was to see if you were at the Flaxseeds', and I don't think I ought to show my face there again. It's bad enough that I'm here in the village."

"Aren't you the prince? Can't you go where you like?"

"Ah, but who can 'like' to face the dour frown of Kendra Flaxseed?" Christian shook his head. "Her frown is still as disapproving as ever, isn't it? I can't imagine that she should change in so short a time."

"I wouldn't say that *disapproving* is the right word for it," Emmazel answered, leaning towards him over the table. "But between her and Mrs. E, visiting that house is almost *terrifying*."

"And we all know how little terrifies the great Emmazel of the tower," said Christian.

Emmazel pulled back, not sure how to answer when there was so *much* of the world that intimidated her. Was he being sarcastic? If he were Night, then that certainly would have been sarcasm. But he wasn't Night.

Night was a *cat*.

And also not here. Why was she even thinking about him right now? No, Christian must be complimenting her, because he didn't know her as well as that cat did.

"Well," Christian continued. "I suppose I should let you return to your business, and I'll explore the market. I'll find you in a few hours and we can talk all about the latest news. Though … you wouldn't happen to have a love potion or two for sale?"

His gaze swept the table, and Emmazel's heart leapt into her throat.

"No, of course not!" she quickly declared, and then she composed herself. "Why? Are you looking for love?"

Christian gave a careless shrug. "Ah, but it seems like just the sort of potion you would make, and it would be wonderfully useful for couples trapped in arranged marriages that they must make the best of."

"Oh. Well, that's pragmatic." Emmazel frowned. "I don't sell love potions. Too irresponsible; they can be so easily misused."

"Ah, but it sounds like you *can* make them?"

"It would also be irresponsible for me to make such a claim." Emmazel shook her head. "Believe what you will; I will say nothing."

"And a gentleman should never pry for a lady's secrets." Christian put on a solemn frown as his gaze swept the table. "And I should probably purchase something, to make up for taking your time. What would you recommend to a young man such as myself?"

Emmazel gulped, glanced down at her wares, and snatched up a bottle. "This one helps improve focus and promotes a clear mind, if you would like it."

"And I need all the clarity of mind I can get, don't I?" And before Emmazel could say another thing, he threw some gold coins down on the counter, snatched up the potion, and carried on his way, pausing only to give Heather a careless wink as she noticed him.

Heather twisted around and grabbed Emmazel's arm. "Was that…"

Emmazel nodded and pushed the coins towards her. "Yes,

it was the prince. He'll return after we're done because he came to visit, but didn't want to distract us from our business."

"How many potions did he buy?" breathed Heather as she counted the coins.

"One," Emmazel answered. "Did he pay too much? You tell me that I'm supposed to try to get as much for every potion as people are willing to pay. But it is usually silver coins…"

Heather looked up from the coins to stare at Emmazel, then shook her head. "Well, he's a prince. I suppose he can afford generosity." Then she quickly swept the coins into the box with the rest of their earnings for the day.

The rest of day went well, and they sold most of their wares. Emmazel saw Christian a few more times, wandering through the market, chatting and laughing. He really was a prince charming.

At the end of it all, Heather and Emmazel closed up the table, put their unsold wares away, and then made their own purchases for the week.

Christian caught up with them as they bargained for the flour. Well, Heather bargained.

"Ah, there you are! Finished already? My, but this day has gone by so quickly!"

Emmazel laughed, shifting the weight of her basket. "Well, we still need to walk home, but all of the sitting around, trying to convince people that my syrups will cure their coughs is over. Until next week."

"Ah, yes, I feel the same after every session of court." Christian shook his head. "Now, that basket looks heavy, and I imagine that you only plan to add more to it before you head home, based on your companion's current employment."

"The miller typically delivers the flour to the tower for us," said Emmazel. "It's more than we can carry, so we pay extra for the service. We carry pretty much everything else home ourselves, though." And Heather, like each of Emmazel's companions before her, used to carry it home by herself.

"Then I must insist that you allow me to offer my services," said Christian. "It would be terribly remiss for me to escort you home and make you carry everything yourself. No, I shall fetch my horse from the stables at once and volunteer him to the cause."

"For a moment, I thought you were planning to carry this basket yourself." Emmazel arched an eyebrow.

"The thought crossed my mind," said Christian. "Until I remembered I had a horse."

Emmazel laughed as he disappeared back into the crowd. Heather finished with the miller and rejoined Emmazel.

"That was the last one," Heather declared. "So, where do you think the prince is? Since you said he wanted to talk after we were done."

"He's getting his horse," Emmazel answered. "Perhaps we can meet him at the stable? Do you know where the stable is?"

Heather laughed. "Of course. Follow me."

They met Christian as he was leaving the stable, and he lit into a smile. "Ah! Good! I was dreading looking for you in that crowd again, but here you are! Let's load up, shall we?"

Emmazel quite happily relinquished her basket, glad to be free of the weight. Heather insisted that she keep hold of the eggs but was more than willing to let Christian take the rest of her supplies.

As the Prince tied up the last of the apples, Heather gave a sudden gasp and pressed herself against the stable wall. "It's Farmer Marin!" she gasped.

Emmazel swung around to face the direction of Heather's wide-eyed stare. A lanky young man had just emerged from the stable, leading a dusty gray mule laden with a few baskets of his own. He was handsome enough – Emmazel could see why Heather's head had been turned. Still, his clothes were worn and dirty, and Emmazel *hoped* that that wasn't meant to be his *best* shirt.

Then his gaze swung their way, and a strange expression lit his features as he saw Heather. His jaw worked, as though he was about to say something.

Christian glanced from one to the other, then lit into a grin, stepped towards the man, and held out his hand. "Farmer

Marin, eh? It's good to meet you."

"Hello, yes," said the farmer, hesitantly accepting the offered hand and shaking it. "Who would you be? I've not seen you around these parts."

"He's Prince Christian!" blurted Heather, peeling herself away from the wall.

"Prince!" repeated Farmer Marin, going stiff. He quickly dropped Christian's hand and took a step back. "I didn't – I mean, what can I do for you?"

"Continue your good work, is all," Prince Christian instructed. "I've always admired farmers such as yourself."

"I see. Well." Farmer Marin swallowed as he glanced from Christian to Heather to Emmazel. "I had heard that you had left your tower, Miss. Never thought I'd ever see you with my own eyes. Not up close like this, at any rate. I – I ought to be getting home to my sisters. I wish you well, all of you."

He clucked at his mule, and they carried on, though his gaze lingered on Heather. Emmazel's stomach twisted. He loved her. She knew that syrupy expression on a man's face. All this time, and he still cared for the girl who had so cruelly rejected him.

And it had been cruel. Emmazel had made sure of it in her attempt to break them apart.

"Well, we should be on our way as well, shouldn't we, ladies?" asked Christian. "Ah, but today was a good day. I should get out like this more often. Get to know my people. It's what a good future king should do, yes?"

"I imagine it would be," said Heather. "I think you'll make a wonderful king. Though, really, I'm just an orphan found on a doorstep, so what do I know?"

"I've always thought that orphans found on doorsteps have the best opinions of all," said Christian. "For if they are well-treated and happy with their lot, then things really are at peace, yes?"

"Oh, I quite agree," said Emmazel, nodding. "And this is why you're going to make an excellent king. You know, I almost didn't believe that you would return – not any time soon, at least. I certainly hoped and dreamed, but you're the *prince*! You have duties to attend to – I didn't dare expect it!"

Christian laughed. "Well, I could hardly stay away once I learned that such lovely young ladies live here. Besides, no other nobleman has ever visited your tower and been able to stay away afterward, so why should I be any different?"

"Why indeed?" Emmazel smiled to herself – this was going so brilliantly well. And all without a love potion!

"Tell me – is Kendra Flaxseed a frequent visitor to these markets?" Christian continued. "She was here today, at any rate, and I should hate to think that I just have such ill luck. She had some choice words for me, too! Must be growing bold, having returned to her native land."

"I've rarely seen her at market, but I also didn't see her today." Emmazel frowned. Well, even *she* would hesitate to call them *proper* friends. Even if she came to market, there was no reason to expect that she would need Emmazel's potions. "I would have loved to see your meeting, though. She's always been so … *reserved,* so long as I've known her."

"Indeed, indeed," said Christian. "And that answer is fair enough. You have your business to attend to."

"I do, yes." Emmazel shrugged it off. "We're planning a visit to Boxill next week, and she'll be with us."

"After the way she fled our illustrious city?"

"Well, she plans to stay in the background, but Mrs. E wants someone there who knows their way around."

"And I wasn't there to offer my own services when the decision was made – alas!" Christian shook his head. "Is it too late to make amends? Just name the day, and I will do everything in my power to clear my schedule and be there. The Gardener is a visiting sovereign. Promoting friendship with her is important."

"All for her, and nothing about wanting to spend time with Heather and I?"

"A prince can have ulterior motives." Christian sent her a wink. "It's always best when diplomacy means spending time with beautiful young ladies."

Emmazel grinned in satisfaction, glancing towards Heather. "In that case, I'm sure we would be glad of your company. Oh! But it's so strange to think of, after I have lived in my tower for so long. I once thought I would never leave it. I thought it wasn't safe out here for me. I still wonder…"

She lifted her gaze towards the tower, looming on the horizon. It was one thing to venture into the village that had lived in her shadow and had already accepted her as one of their own, even so far as to name itself for her. But in Boxill…

"You have done quite well thus far, and anywhere would only be all the brighter for your presence," said Christian. "It's admirable, really."

Night waited for them as they reached the top of the tower. He sat in Emmazel's chair, tail wrapped around himself as he stared at them with his eyes half-lidded. "So, the prince has returned, and he's brought you back here himself. How valiant of him."

"I thought so," said Emmazel.

Night made a growling noise in the back of his throat but said nothing before he jumped down from the seat and bounded up the stairs.

"Night!" Emmazel shouted after him. She glanced down at her basket, then to Heather, before she ran up the stairs, too. "Night!" she called again. "Don't you run off on me like that. What was that about?"

She reached the apothecary to find him turned to face her in the middle of the room in a defensive posture.

"Night?" She tilted her head to the side quizzically. "Night, I know you have never liked any of the noblemen who have ever visited, but this is ridiculous."

"Most every other nobleman has not been the crown prince," Night answered, composing himself slightly – his back was no longer arched, "who you have confessed would tempt you if he were to visit. And now here he is. Tempting you."

"And? I'm not confined to my tower anymore."

"Exactly." Night's tail lashed back and forth. "Now you're free to flirt and laugh to your heart's content."

"Which I've always done if I thought it would inspire greater confidence – you're jealous!"

Night's ears went back. "Me?"

"Yes, you!" Emmazel laughed and scooped him up before he could protest. "And I can't for a moment imagine why! You're a cat, after all! But don't you worry – if I should become queen of Howsill, you will not be forgotten. I shall take you with me as my chief advisor and loyal companion, and you will continue to criticize my every move, as you have always done. And I shall scratch you between the ears and laugh, as I have always done."

Night hung limp in her arms. "Why would I be jealous of that prince? He has to wear clothes and kiss babies. He can hardly sneeze without the approval of the court. Why should a cat, with the freedom to go where he likes and never worry what any man thinks of him, be jealous of a prince?"

"Exactly," said Emmazel. She scratched him behind the ears and sat down in a chair that stood at hand. "You really are a silly cat sometimes, you know that, Night?"

"Indeed, indeed." Night laid his head sullenly on his paws. "Such a silly cat."

"And you're being particularly ridiculous right now." Emmazel tapped his nose. "I've only ever said that Prince Christian would tempt me, not that he would steal my heart. I'm sure there are other, far better reasons for him to be here, in Hightower. So don't worry yourself about it. Let's go back downstairs and help Heather put the supplies away, yes?"

Night had closed his eyes and begun purring.

Emmazel shook her head. "You would be frightful as a palace cat, you know. You would be downright spoiled, and you would love every moment of it."

"You will never see me as a spoiled housecat," said Night. "'Twould be blasphemy."

"But just think of all the exotic fish you would be given to eat!"

"There's more to life than exotic fish."

"So you say." Emmazel released a long sigh as her thoughts turned pensive. "Christian offered to meet us when we visit Boxill."

"Ah. Enjoy yourself, then."

"Night … would you be willing to come to Boxill with us? I know you don't like her either, but neither do I, and you do like both Heather and me, and we're both going. So, will you come with me? It will make everything so much better if you're there. I…"

"You're still scared of the outside world," said Night. "Very well. I'll come with you – but don't expect me to say a word. Boxill is a large city. They wouldn't know what to do with a talking cat."

"No, they wouldn't." Emmazel gave him an extra-good scratch under the chin. "But may I point out that you will be traveling with a green woman who has a rose vine growing out of her head?"

"A fair point."

"Thank you. It means everything to me."

"That's why I'll do it," said Night. "That and the fact your father won't be going to keep an eye on you."

For once, such a jab didn't sting, like it usually did.

~

The day of their venture came, and it found Emmazel trapped in the carriage, next to Kendra, across from the family of E's, and with Night in her lap. Heather had opted to ride on the box with the driver, which no one protested. Everything was still too awkward between her and Sir E for them to sit comfortably in the same carriage.

Foxglove was not with them. Their father had taken ill that morning, and she had offered to stay behind to care for him. And, really, it had been more of a "downright insist" than an offer. Emmazel had wanted to stay herself, but no, here she was in this carriage. There had never been room for Foxglove on the trip, anyway.

The silence in the carriage was terribly awkward, especially as Emmazel kept hearing those unspoken conversations pass between Mrs. E and her husband. Terribly rude of them to go on like that. They weren't the only ones in the carriage, after all, and *some* parties had never traveled more than a mile in their life and really needed a distraction right now.

Why couldn't it be Sir E on the box? Heather would know exactly what to say to put everyone at ease. Or, at least … she would say *something*.

The more the two spoke, the better Emmazel understood the unspoken conversation between the E's. She still couldn't make out anything clearly, but they discussed Hansel's ability to shift forms, as they still didn't understand it.

As though he heard himself being talked about – and it was likely he did – Hansel suddenly shifted into the form of a dog again and started barking at Night. Night instinctively recoiled, arching his back and hissing. Kendra's eyes widened in a panic, but she said nothing – she had likely seen the boy shift before.

"Hansel! Enough of that!" Sir E ordered, pulling his canine-shaped son close to whisper sternly in his ear. Night collected himself, settled back into Emmazel's lap, and licked his paw indignantly.

Mrs. E covered her eyes as she gave another one of those long, tired sighs of hers. "I'm so sorry about that. He does it at the worst times."

"He caught me by surprise, that's all, and I reacted as a cat would," said Night, licking harder. "As your son, it's only natural he would be so strong, and he's at the age of impulsive experimentation."

Mrs. E removed her hand from her eyes and stared, blinking at the cat. "You … find this natural? And it is from me and not his father?"

Night turned his head to stare at her coolly. "You *don't* find this natural? I know that knowledge was obscured and confused in your grandmother's reign, but you have access to the Forest's memories."

"Not at the moment, and it's jumbled confusion when I

do," Mrs. E explained. "Unless I seek out information, I don't retain it – and Hansel only *just* started doing this. Even when I do seek information, well, the Forest waited five years before it gave me any knowledge about Howsill and let Earnest discover Emmazel." She shook her head. "My grandmother hid from a lot of her own actions, and it's been easier said than done to make sense of it all."

"Ah. Naturally." Night's tail flicked. "Well, it's from both of you, simply put. And it's natural enough for one of his kind, though rare. Most Sensitive men can't shift on whim like he can, but he's your son, and the Forest's magic runs through his veins. He'll have to be especially reckless or anger someone particularly powerful to find himself trapped in the wrong form, like his father and uncle were."

Sir E sat up straighter. "Barend and I were cursed by the Mistress because Barend reacted badly to learning that the girl he liked was a Frost."

"Please. You really think that the Mistress had the power to turn men into beasts? Her power was *plants*." Night's tail lashed right into Emmazel's face. "Magic can be latent enough in a person's blood as to be almost imperceptible, and it's more common than anyone realizes. A girl whose skin is just a bit too cool to the touch but is never bothered by the cold. A man who can shape whatever he wants with metal, no matter how impossible. A woman who can make anything grow. A young boy with an inexplicable bond with his dog or horse. Were you or your brother good with animals before falling foul of the Mistress?"

"Not remarkably so, but I know I always thought that animals understood me better than humans ever would. Except Darren. Darren was a good friend but also more anti-social than I was, so I'm not sure he counted." Earnest's frown grew thoughtful as he scratched Hansel behind the ears. "But I never would have thought … we long suspected a Wood Spirit ancestor in my mother's family."

"Sensitive magic can generally be traced to a Wood Spirit. The Mistress was power hungry," Night continued, his tail lashing so hard it hit Emmazel in the face. "And she learned how to steal magic from her fellow Sensitives. It left women weak and empty, but men – oh, men were her masterpiece. She would push them into the form of a beast and then steal their magic, trapping them there. Those who didn't have enough magic to shift on their own, she gave them the difference, pushed them over, and then took everything. She made an art of it. Considered it a game. She hunted men with even the smallest drop of magic, and soon it wasn't even about the power. She just had a morbid desire to destroy men. Is it any wonder that she chose a Zephyr as her husband? Is it any wonder why he *left* her? She ran out of Sensitive men at least thirty years ago, so when your brother stumbled upon her mercy, well!"

"And what happened to all of those men?" Elinrose's hand was over her eyes again. "Always *just* when I think I've found the end of her mess."

"Most of them have probably lost themselves to the beast and lost their lives as well. Some … may have been resourceful enough to have escaped and hidden themselves, but I don't have high hopes of it. It takes … would take severe mental fortitude and self-control. But … this Lilly set Earnest free – she must have been a Sensitive herself to have done it – and you freed your brother-in-law, Gardener, so that's all taken care of. Pat yourself on the back and call it a good day's work."

"Night, we told you—"

"And I told you that I don't need or want anything from you," Night snapped back at her. "I'll accept help from one person and one person only."

Mrs. E's eyebrow rose. "Oh? And whose help would that be? The lovely young lady who—"

"She's dead." Night cut her off. "You might be the great, powerful Gardener with a whole Forest at your command, but even you can't raise the dead. No, don't worry about me. Live your life. Raise your family. Your grandmother was a monster who destroyed countless people, but that's the past. You might have inherited her legacy, but if you waste all of your energy chasing the messes she left behind, you'll never find them all. You have a beautiful son and daughter. Treasure them. You never know what you have until it's gone."

"Perhaps so." Mrs. E stared up at her husband, chewing her lip, then she collapsed against his shoulder. "But … you're here. I'm here. Why can't you just let me fix what I can?"

"Because some things are too broken to fix." Night's tail hit Emmazel in the face again. "Accept it."

"I'm sorry."

"I know you are, and I commend you for it. If it makes you feel any better, I'm sorry too. And I've been sorry for a very long time."

Silence fell, broken only as Kendra caught her breath. "The cat talks?"

Emmazel swallowed. "Yes, the cat talks. He's been able to for a while. Consider yourself lucky to join this special circle. Or don't. As you just heard, he can be so … morbid."

Night's tail hit her in the face a third time.

Silence again, even more uncomfortable than before. Even the E's barely spoke to each other.

Night's story. What the Mistress did to all of those men. Emmazel's *mother*.

"I can't do this," she finally blurted, shaking her head as she hugged the cat close.

"Do what?" asked Sir E.

"*This*. This trip. Facing people. A new place. How are we supposed to make this trip to Boxill with all of *this* hanging over us?"

"I'm sorry," said Night. "I shouldn't have said any of that, but she wanted to know."

"We can't just stop now," said Kendra. "We made all of the plans and arrangements. The *prince* is going to meet us."

"Emmazel is right," said Mrs. E, lifting her head again. "That was a lot to take in. We should … consider taking a short break. Stepping outside. Getting fresh air. Stretching our legs."

"That's a good idea," said Emmazel. "I like that idea." Best idea the woman had ever had.

Sir E called for the carriage to stop, and Emmazel breathed a sigh of relief and *slightly* loosened her hold on Night.

"Why are we stopping?" asked Heather as Sir E exited the carriage.

"Hansel needed to get out and run," he answered, watching his son scamper into the grass. "Little boys aren't made for spending hours in a carriage. Especially not when they want to be a dog most of the time."

Heather blinked. "Okay."

"Also, I got nerves, and I don't think I can face a whole city of people," added Emmazel as Sir E handed her down from the carriage.

Heather shook her head and actually rolled her eyes. "You've had nerves ever since the Gardener proposed this trip. As *I* keep telling you, you just need to push through and get it over with."

Night jumped down from Emmazel's arms and darted out into the grass, disappearing into the trees beyond.

Mrs. E's gaze fixed on the treeline. "There are wild strawberries ahead – we could go pick them and make a day of that instead of our trip to Boxill."

"I like that idea, too," said Emmazel. "And I think Night already had it."

"It's decided, then," said Mrs. E. "Strawberries."

**23**     "But what about the prince?" Kendra protested, still lingering in the carriage doorway. "He's expecting us. "We can't just abandon him for strawberries, now can we? It would be inappropriate."

"True enough," said Mrs. E, glancing up at her husband.

"I can ride ahead and inform him of our change of plans," Sir E volunteered. "We are only a few more miles from Boxill. Perhaps he would like to return and join us for strawberries. You can come with me if it means so much to you."

Kendra's lips pressed into a line as she considered. "Very well. But you must be aware how irregular all of this is."

"Oh, definitely," said Sir E. "I know quite well the demands of royal life. Still, when a maiden is in distress, plans must be changed, which I think he will completely understand."

Kendra disappeared back into the carriage.

"I shall return, then," said Sir E, before he pulled his wife into a tight hug and pressed a kiss into her hair. She buried her face in his chest for a long moment, then pulled back and let him take a kiss from her lips.

Emmazel wrinkled her nose. They looked just *so* syrupy sweet together – but, then, they were married. Wasn't this exactly how things should be in marriage?

"Make sure that Hansel doesn't spend too much time chasing Night," Sir E instructed as he pulled back. "That cat has been through enough.”

“Agreed. Be safe.” Mrs. E then added something silent – the impression of which, Emmazel was fairly sure her niece hadn’t meant for it to be overheard. Then Sir E climbed back into the carriage with Kendra, and the two were off.

Emmazel inched towards her niece. “I don’t know how you two do it, but I think you should know I hear when you and your husband talk like that.”

Mrs. E arched an eyebrow. “Oh, can you? How interesting. I’ve wondered, given your strength – but you also block so much out, I couldn’t be sure.”

“And yet you kept doing it?” Emmazel frowned.

“You’ve never said anything about it, even when I said some very pointed things. You sometimes react *when* I do it, but it’s never specifically to what I say.” Mrs. E gave an unspoken order to a nearby tree, and its branches wove into baskets.

“Well, I don’t hear *what* you say, just that you’re talking,” Emmazel confessed. “But the more I hear you do it, the clearer it gets, and now I get the general gist – or at least the topic of the conversation.”

“Ah.” Mrs. E plucked one of the baskets from the tree. “Then it sounds like you’re lowering your guard and improving your ability to process information. Congratulations.” *Now can you hear me when I speak to you directly?*

Emmazel sucked in a breath. “I heard that, yes.”

Mrs. E nodded. *It’s the language of the Wood Spirits,* she explained. *Strong Sensitives can hear and speak it, and Earnest and I use it for private conversations. Including flirting, yes.*

“And since I can hear you now?”

“I can help you learn, if you would like.” Mrs. E shifted Ela in her arms. “But not today. We’re both too out of sorts. Let’s go pick strawberries.” *And maybe you don’t want to hear it from me, and maybe you won’t believe me, but you are no more your mother than I am. If Night doesn’t want me to take what he said personally, he certainly doesn’t want you to, either.*

With that, Mrs. E plunged into the tree line. “I think I have enough baskets for everyone, Christian included. Go ahead and hand them out if you want."

Emmazel stared after her for a long moment and then twisted around to see that she was alone. Swallowing, she grabbed one of the baskets and plunged into the trees herself to seek the strawberries.

She'd overreacted, hadn't she? Night's story had been horrible and terrible and awful, but it was no reason for her to have canceled this whole trip. Christian would be disappointed in her, wouldn't he? And poor Heather! She should be the one in the carriage right now, not Kendra! And would Christian choose to return with Sir E when he had to travel in the carriage with the daughter of his family's chief rivals!

This was a mess from every angle.

She should have never left her tower. She should never have made a game of finding love for her companions. She should have stayed content with her life, making cough syrups and fertility potions.

It should have stopped at Isolde.

But strawberries were a good distraction, and so, when she found a patch, she knelt and began picking with a vengeance.

~

Emmazel had filled her basket before she found any of her party again – before she stumbled upon Heather and Night tucked together in conversation. She swallowed, shoving down a pang of … not jealousy, because she wasn't jealous.

Heather rushed over and threw her arms around Emmazel's neck. "I'm so sorry! Night explained everything! Well, not everything – he didn't tell me what he told you, because he said he didn't want to talk about it again – but he did explain that he said things about your mother that upset both you and the Gardener a lot. So I now understand why you didn't want to go to Boxill."

Emmazel gave a half-hearted smile and hugged Heather back. "I hope, if we ever find answers about your parents, it'll be so much better than the answers I got about my mother."

"I can't imagine that I can find out anything worse." Heather gave a long sigh and pulled back. "But, you never know. I could find out that my father was a notorious thief and murderer, and he thrust me upon the blacksmith because I was a burden, slowed him down, and he never loved me." Her nose wrinkled. "It's really hard to come up with a story worse than the Mistress, and I *have* tried."

"I appreciate the attempt." Emmazel laughed weakly. "So, how has your strawberry picking gone? Because I've got enough for several jams, at least, and maybe a cake or two."

"That sounds delicious," said Heather. "I've not picked nearly as many, I'm afraid. "I was too distracted trying to find Night and discover what had happened in the carriage. Sorry."

"It's fine." Emmazel took a deep breath. "Maybe we should head back to the road and see if Sir E has returned with Kendra and if the prince is with them."

"Of course the prince will be with them," muttered Night. "Why would he turn down an opportunity to flirt?"

"Night!" Emmazel rolled her eyes. "Enough of that."

"Don't worry, I don't plan to say anything of the sort to his face." Night flicked his tail as he walked past them. "I don't plan to say a word to him at all."

"That's because he doesn't want Christian to know he's a talking cat," Emmazel told Heather, shaking her head. "He has to protect his secret, after all. Has to be careful who hears him speak."

"Right." Heather nodded. "Are things always like this between you and Night? Because you argue almost constantly."

"Live in a tower with a snarky, talking cat for over twenty years, and soon you run out of polite conversation and move on to friendly jabs." Emmazel shrugged and followed the cat. "Besides, he almost always starts it."

"It's a little bit ridiculous, but I suppose, given both of your situations, it's only natural. If a bit sad."

The carriage was not at the road when they reached it, though Mrs. E was, sitting in the grass, staring at the road. Hansel ran in circles around her, still a puppy, and Ela lay in another woven cradle.

"Tired of strawberries already?" Emmazel asked.

"Ela was, and I figured three baskets was enough," said Mrs. E. "Had to leave some strawberries for Kendra and Christian, after all."

"Three," Emmazel repeated, setting her basket next to Mrs. E's collection. "I don't know whether to be scared or impressed."

"It's just strawberries," said Mrs. E, shrugging. "But I guess I did get a bit carried away."

"How much longer do you think it'll be before they return?" asked Heather, frowning back over her shoulder. Night had disappeared back into the trees.

"It depends on if they encountered any troubles and how long it takes them to explain to Christian," said Mrs. E. "But it should be soon."

Emmazel sat down on the grass next to Mrs. E. "What are we going to do about ... what Night said in the carriage."

"Given that it doesn't sound like there's much I can do ... not be the Mistress. Which is what I've been trying to do for the last five years, and I've mostly succeeded. I mean, I have her power, but I like to think I use it for good, but sometimes, I wonder, whatever I do – will it be enough? Will it *ever* be enough?"

Emmazel opened her mouth, but before she could make a single comment – encouraging or scathing – she heard the carriage, and it came to a stop in front of them, just moments later.

"Ah, good, here we are," said Sir E, emerging from the carriage. "I was worried that we might miss the spot, but how could anyone miss such lovely ladies waiting for us?"

"Amazing," said Christian, stepping out after him. "I suppose it was the least they could do, after they changed all of the plans, yes?"

"Of course it was," said Kendra as Sir E handed her down from the carriage. "And now, since I'm here, I guess I'll go pick some strawberries."

She marched past Emmazel and Mrs. E, snatched up one of the baskets, and plunged into the woods.

"I'm sorry about all of the trouble," said Emmazel, dipping her head. "I just—"

"Don't worry." Christian raised his hands disarmingly. "Earnest already explained the situation, and I completely understand. Strange to think of – magic like that. For so long, that sort of thing was thought to be mere legend and myth – the closest we had to magic was rumors of the Forest and you, but to know that it actually happened, well! I don't envy your family history, even compared to my own situation."

"He told you … *everything?*"

"Well, perhaps not everything – but he seemed pretty upset by the situation himself and was rambling about it pretty badly," Christian confessed. "But he also repeated himself and went in circles, and I soon got lost in it. Besides, Kendra was frowning at me."

"Ah."

"Her frowns are not to be underestimated."

"Oh, I know." Emmazel laughed. "But, really, I am sorry about the inconvenience – I know you had so many plans for us today."

"And I still have plans. Eating strawberries, for one. And secondly, to invite you and your companions to continue on back with me to Boxill tonight and not return home until tomorrow, at least. Westbrook is visiting, you see, and I know how close you are to his wife. I would hate for you to miss them."

"That sounds … acceptable, if everyone else is fine with it." Emmazel nodded. "I should have asked Anna to come with us on the trip from the start."

"It's decided then."

## 24

The last few miles to Boxill were even more cramped than before, but they made it there with eight baskets of strawberries that were handed off to the palace cook for breakfast the next morning. Emmazel gaped at the buildings – many as tall as her tower, but so much larger, and so many of them, packed even more tightly than the village.

The palace was the largest building of all, and they rode right up to it and through the massive gates. Heather's eyes were wider than Emmazel's as they disembarked the carriage, making Emmazel feel better about the way she was staring.

After breaking up to and following servants to rooms where they were allowed to freshen up after the journey, the group reconvened for dinner. The room was twice the size of the Flaxseeds' dining hall, yet Christian referred to it as one of the *casual* dining halls.

"My parents won't be joining us tonight," he explained. "Eager as they are to meet you, Emmazel, tonight was rather short notice, and they already had other dignitaries to meet with. I'm sure you'll see them at breakfast, though."

Lord Westbrook and Anna were there, though, and that was the important part. Emmazel sat between Anna and Heather, Night still in her lap, as she tried to ignore the stares of the servants. The witch of the tower had a reputation to maintain, or so Christian claimed. Emmazel thought it ridiculous, but at least it gave her an excuse to keep her cat nearby.

She needed Night right now.

"It is so good to see you here, Emmazel," Anna said over soup. "I've dreamed of this for so long – or at least, ever since I married Westbrook. You're a natural here, just as I've always known."

Emmazel took a sip, *not* feeling like a natural.

Mrs. E, laughing at the other end of the table with Sir E and Prince Christian, was the natural. She was a princess, after all. A princess and the Gardener. Everything that Emmazel would never be.

What even was her purpose? Had it only ever been to live, locked in a tower while her mother terrorized her people, emerging only after everything was put to right by someone else? And it hadn't even been a dashing knight who had "saved" her. It was infuriating.

At least Night had some fish to keep him happy as he sat in her lap. It had been the price of his presence, and she considered it a small price to pay.

"I can't believe anyone could live in a place like this," said Heather. "The whole village could fit in here twice over, and you wouldn't even notice!"

"Well, between servants and visiting and resident nobility, a few villages-worth of people *do* live here," said Anna. "But I agree that this is all so strange to think of. How did you and I find our way here, Heather? It's only natural that Emmazel's path would take this turn – she's Emmazel – but us!"

"I never expected to leave my tower," Emmazel pointed out. "Both of you knew, when my father chose you as my companions, that it would likely result in your marriage into the nobility. The only destiny I was ever meant to have has gone to my niece."

Servants cleared away the soup bowls and replaced them with salad. Emmazel watched Anna to see which fork she was supposed to use.

"So, all that means is you can choose your own destiny

now." Anna reached over and patted Emmazel's hand. "Once upon a time, I thought I would marry a nice farmer, have a whole pack of children, and live my life out as the most common woman imaginable. But that didn't happen. I thought the world would pass me by – but it didn't. I took my destiny into my own hands, accepted by your father's request that I serve as your companion."

"And I commend you for the initiative," said Emmazel. "But you *did* have a witch of the tower to turn to. I don't."

"You have me, so don't you worry," Anna assured her.

"I thought you were happy to live alone in your tower," said Heather.

"Yes, but that was before I left my tower and found out about my mother. Don't worry about me. I'll figure something out eventually."

"Of course you will – you work miracles, dear Emmazel," said Anna. "And I have every confidence that you will fight for your own happily ever after with at least as much drive as you had for ours."

The salad was taken away and replaced with a small bit of pastry filled with meat. Emmazel's plate had an extra pastry, which she slipped to Night.

"You're in the business of miracles, says Lady Anna?" asked Christian, leaning back in his seat to send Emmazel a raised eyebrow. "I could use a miracle, as I might have mentioned before. My parents are pressuring me to marry, and the girl they've picked is, well, far be it from me to talk ill of any young lady, but to have her as my queen would be the downfall of Howsill, I am convinced."

Emmazel smiled half-heartedly as Night's claws suddenly dug into her leg. "Well, I usually work the other way, finding the perfect gentlemen for my companions, but I can see what I can do. I've left my tower now, so I could branch out."

"Excellent!" Christian slapped his hand against the table. "So, what do you need to start? Shall I describe to you what I seek in a woman? Because I've thought about it a fair bit, and I have a few ideas."

Emmazel tilted her head to the side as she adjusted the position of Night's claws. "It could help, so let's hear it."

Servants cleared away the meat pastry plates and passed out whole quails.

"She must be beautiful, naturally," said Christian, leaning forward eagerly. "I am aware that beauty fades, but it needs to start out well. I'm not particular about the *kind* of beauty, but clear, intelligent eyes are a must. Because she needs to be intelligent. Intelligent, kind, and a shoulder for me to lean on as my queen."

"Noted, and I shall do my very best for you." Emmazel glanced at Heather out of the corner of her eye and grinned broadly.

"I shall rest easier knowing that my future is in safe hands."

Emmazel gave Night an entire leg from her quail to distract him and his claws.

~

The conversation improved now that Emmazel's nerves had recovered. It was amazing what a renewal of purpose could do for the soul. Soon she laughed and chatted as loudly as anyone there.

Dinner finished, and they all moved to a sitting room, where the conversation continued, more freely than before.

"It really is an honor to have you here, Emmazel," Christian announced as he sat on a sofa beside her. "The witch of the tower!"

"The proper term is Sensitive," said Mrs. E. "Emmazel's power, like mine, is hereditary and limited to communicating with plans, and it has nothing to do with witchcraft. Emmazel, perhaps, has a more practical use for it, with her potions, but none of them are anything that any other herbalist couldn't make."

"Some potions require a bit of extra magic," Emmazel confessed. Such as love potions. "But I'm especially careful with those."

Mrs. E's eyebrow flickered.

"Ah, but 'the witch of the tower' has a so much better ring to it," said Christian. "It's a title to lend her mystery – much as your own 'Gardener.'"

"We are trying to remove the stigma surrounding magic, which has grown during the Mistress's reign," explained Mrs. E. "I chose the title Gardener to distance myself from my grandmother, and I assure you that calling Emmazel a 'witch' will only grow the stigma."

"I don't see what it matters to you what I'm called," Emmazel countered, bristling. "You have your Forest to tend to, and I have to find out what else to do with myself. I've spent the last twenty-five years making potions and helping my companions find love, and if people call me a witch because of it, what of it? I'm helping, and that's what matters."

Mrs. E narrowed her eyes. *What matters is that the word bothers you. You hate being called a witch because it reinforces what you fear. The fact that you're different.*

"Get out of my head!" Emmazel flew to her feet, glaring.

"Emma…" Night gave a warning growl.

"I'm not in your head. I'm sorry, Emmazel." Mrs. E cautiously stood, and Emmazel felt the power in the room shift defensively. "I didn't want to speak aloud to spare your feelings."

"Maybe I don't want my feelings spared!" Emmazel pooled all of her power to meet Mrs. E's.

"You don't want to do this." Mrs. E shook her head. "I'm not your enemy."

"I know, but you have everything that was meant to be mine!"

"Emmazel, that doesn't even begin to be true," Night countered. "Yes, she was there to fight the Mistress when you weren't, but do you really need a Forest? It's all just a giant hassle, and you're better off without it."

"That cat talks?" observed Christian.

"Oh, yes, only the best for the witch of the tower," said Sir E, dryly.

"Earnest, you are not helping," said Mrs. E.

"Emmazel, will you please just sit down," said Heather, grabbing at Emmazel's skirts and trying to pull her back. "It's not worth it."

It wasn't. Emmazel knew that. But she was tired. Tired of stepping back and dismissing her feelings. Tired of watching others succeed, knowing that it would never be her turn. Tired of letting the world pass her by.

She wasn't going to let it pass her by a moment more.

"Emmazalea, please don't do this," Mrs. E repeated. "It's been a long day, you received upsetting news, and you're in an unfamiliar place. I know you're upset, and for a lot of good reasons. But I've warned you before that I don't want to fight you. It won't end well for you."

"Nothing ever ends well for me. It ends well for others. Like you. Like every single one of my companions. I just sit back and help it happen."

"And we all appreciate it!" declared Anna.

"Good. I've never resented my companions." Emmazel took another step towards Mrs. E. "Because they were happy, I could be happy – as though they were pieces of me that I could break off and set free. And maybe it wasn't fair that I saw them that way, but I did everything in my power for them. Everything. Because I had lived my whole life in a tower, terrified of the world outside, and tell me what part of that was fair."

"None of it," said Mrs. E. "What happened to you wasn't fair. What happened to Earnest and Barend wasn't fair. What happened to Night wasn't fair. What happened to Lilly and my mother and every Sensitive like them wasn't fair. What happened to this very land wasn't fair. The Mistress didn't deal in 'fair,' and you should thank Austere that your father did everything he could to keep you safe."

"My safety was a prison."

"And you should have been free five years ago. I'm sorry. I tried to find you sooner, I really did, but I think I was too scared. Too scared that finding you would only mean finding myself *here*. Please, let's not fight."

"I don't hate my father. I can't hate him."

"Emmazel, if you are going to fight her, then may I at least recommend that it not be in the crown prince's sitting room," said Night.

Emmazel glanced down at the cat, hovering just beside her, then to Prince Christian, who sat leaned forward, watching with rapt attention. It seemed to her that he was quite content to watch this go down.

And Emmazel was equally content to give him such a show.

"I can't hate my father," she repeated, fixing her gaze back on Mrs. E. "He's been through too much, and he's always done what he could. I can't hate him for letting his fear hold him back from doing more."

"You're a good daughter; of course not." Mrs. E relaxed her stance to give Emmazel a placating smile.

"I can't hate my mother, either. She may have been the greatest villain that ever existed, but that means nothing to me. I lived in a *tower*. My world was walls and fear. I don't know who she was – I just know that you stand in her place when it should have been me."

Mrs. E's posture changed again, and her chin lifted as she regarded Emmazel with a new, thoughtful gaze. "I see. I understand that."

And her acceptance, her lack of hostility, was the worst part of all. How dare she – how *dare* she just stand there, staring with sympathy instead of fear. As though Emmazel was a helpless puppy instead of an equal.

"Please, just sit down, Emmazel!" cried Heather. "You don't need the Forest. You have us!"

"Except I do think she needs this," said Mrs. E. Her power surged forward as she closed the distance between them and grabbed Emmazel's hand.

All of Emmazel's senses inverted.

**25** They were in that Forest again. Not physically – Emmazel was still vaguely aware of her body in the palace sitting room – but in her mind's eye, she and Mrs. E stood circling each other in a forest clearing.

"You don't hate me," said Mrs. E, pooling power in her hands. "You hate that you no longer have walls to hide behind and to tell you what's yours and what's forbidden. I removed the villain who kept you from leaving the tower. I gave you a way out of your prison, and you don't know what to do with freedom. You hate me because I broke your world wide open and now you have to make choices."

Emmazel narrowed her eyes as she centered herself in this strange pseudo-reality. "My world was fine. It would have been fine forever, but then you had to go and ruin everything!"

"You might have been fine, but the world wasn't. My sister was *dying,* and I did what I had to do."

Emmazel shook her head. "Keep telling yourself that."

"Emmazel, the world isn't that simple, and it doesn't fit nicely into boxes," Mrs. E answered. "I didn't break your world; I just opened the door and made you face how big it really was."

"My father is dying because of you."

"He's lived a long life, and this was a price he knew he would have to pay. Nothing lasts forever." Mrs. E sighed, lowering her guard. "I wish it had been otherwise. I lost my own father right before it started, and it still hurts every time I realize he's gone. I don't wish that on you, and if there had been any other way, I would have taken it, but I did what I had to do to protect the people I care about."

"And where does that leave me?"

"Free."

Emmazel took a step forward. "I don't feel free."

"That's because it's new. It scares you to have an open door. Now, I brought you here so you can act on your hurt and anger. Scream. Shout. Rail against the walls that have held you in your whole life. I'm the face you've given the villains in your life? Fine. So be it. Fight me."

"I…" Emmazel drew up short and threw up her hands. "How is that supposed to help me?"

"It's what you want to do." Mrs. E shrugged. "I don't know how it will help, but you'll still be making your own choice."

"By doing what you tell me to do!"

Mrs. E took a sharp breath and took a step back. "Very well then, but you're the one on the offensive."

Emmazel screamed and threw her magic forward. "Stop it!"

"Easily enough," said Mrs. E, raising her magic to deflect Emmazel's. "That was good! You're powerful, Emma! It's beautiful!"

"Can't you at least *act* like you're scared of me?" Emmazel threw another wave of magic.

"Then fight harder. Throw yourself into it!" Mrs. E deflected that wave easily as well. "And look yourself in the mirror and face your fear. Why do you hate me so much?"

"You have your own ideas about it," said Emmazel.

"And I've said them, but now I think it's time that you say yours. Now, be honest with yourself. We can't fix something if we don't know the source of the problem."

"You stole my throne!"

"Emmazel, look me in the eye and tell me that you were

ever going to claim it."

Emmazel's breath caught, then she flung back, "How was I supposed to claim what I didn't even know existed? Sometimes I wonder if my father ever planned to tell me about my mother. He certainly seemed content to not say a word about it until your husband showed up to *investigate*."

"Fair enough," said Mrs. E. "But imagine for a moment that he had told you, before I ventured into the Forest, and it bullied me into becoming the Gardener. Or if I never stepped foot in the Forest at all. I almost didn't. I had common sense. What would you have done then?"

Emmazel threw down another wave of magic, this one sending a dozen thick vines to wrap around Mrs. E. But Mrs. E caught them and turned them away.

"Come on, Emmazalea," she taunted. "Tell me. Tell yourself. Would you have ever left your tower to save a Forest you didn't know?"

"I'd like to think I would have!"

"But you don't know." Mrs. took a deep breath and adjusted her stance back into a defensive posture. "I think, deep down, you're afraid that you would have been a coward and stayed in that tower, even knowing that thousands suffered because of your inaction. You hate me because I took action – but I am no better than you, I promise. I was willing and ready to walk away from that Forest and let it be someone else's problem. I tried so hard to escape.

"But I never would have lived with myself if Snowmari had died. I think the Forest would have found your weakness, too, if I hadn't been there. It knew about you. Earnest said you were having dreams until it found me. It would have only been a matter of time."

"Nice speech. But you're still the one who won, and I'm still left with nothing."

"That attitude is exactly what corrupted your mother." The humor fell from Mrs. E's voice. "Maybe it is better that you stayed in your tower. Power would have destroyed you."

"I'm every bit as good as you, Elinrose!" Emmazel shouted.

"I should be the one standing where you are, and it was only a cruel twist of fate that kept me from it."

"Emma…"

"No. Don't 'Emma' me. You didn't want the Forest? Fine! Maybe you never deserved it."

And with that, Emmazel surged forward and latched onto Mrs. E's power.

~

Elinrose's memories surged through Emmazel with her power. Memories of ice and snow and love.

"I'm going to fight for all of that, I hope you understand, Emmazel," Elinrose warned, tightening her hold. "My very life hangs in the balance, and I am not letting you take that from me."

Emmazel squeezed her eyes shut, trying to block out the hopeful eyes of a twelve-year-old girl but not succeeding.

"My niece, Mayblossom," Elinrose explained. "Her mother died at her birth, so Snowmari and I were the ones to raise her. Mostly me."

Snowmari was a prominent fixture in Elinrose's memories as well. Her Frost sister who had married Earnest's older brother. How awkward that had to be!

Snowmari led to thoughts of Faia, their Frost sister-in-law, Mayblossom's stepmother, and to James, their brother. Elirnose didn't get to see either of them nearly as much as she wished. She worried over her brother often, but she was proud of him.

She had more friends. Lilly, the Sensitive girl that Earnest had nearly married and who now acted as Elinrose's right hand. Lizzy, their Cinder cousin who was now queen of a whole country of Cinders.

Lilly seemed vaguely familiar, but Emmazel pushed that thought aside. She had to focus.

"It's not fair. You had all of that while I have nothing!"

"You don't have nothing, Emmazel. I am not your enemy. Open your eyes and accept the love that surrounds you. Please.

You and I both have so much to live for, and you can still pull back without hurting us. But don't make me actually fight you."

Emmazel pulled harder.

"Please. Stop. You don't want to do this, and since we're not in the Forest, I don't even want to think about how dangerous the transition could be."

"Maybe you should have thought about that before you decided to fight me," said Emmazel, pulling more and more of Elinrose's magic. It felt good. It made the world feel right.

"Emmazel, this is your last chance. Please just stop."

"But I can't. I have to do this."

Elinrose's eyes lit, and her stance shifted. Now *she* was pulling, her magic shaped like thorny vines. She pulled hard. It hurt. Emmazel thought she was going to break into pieces.

"You aren't going to take everything from me," Elinrose growled. "I fought too hard to get to where I am now."

Emmazel's own world spun, and images of her own life flashed before her eyes. Treasured memories of her father, her companions, and Night.

Oh, Night. He really always had been there, hadn't he?

And her plants. She had spent so much time and poured so much energy into all of them. They had kept her sane through all the years.

Emmazel dug her feet into the ground, refusing to budge. Even as hard as Elinrose pulled, Emmazel still gained ground, inch by inch. Deeper and deeper dug Elinrose's thorns, but she still wasn't strong enough.

"You really, *really* should be scared of me," Emmazel hissed. "You shouldn't have taken what didn't belong to you. The Forest is mine, and—"

Elinrose wasn't alone. Earnest stood behind her, and his strength entwined with hers. The thorns wrapped around Emmazel, ripping her apart.

The world went dark.

## 26

Emmazel was in bed. The world was oddly quiet, as though she were in the tower again, but with an overwhelming sense of emptiness instead of suffocation. Her eyes flew open, but the world remained dark. Panicked, she tried to sit up,

"Easy there. Good. You're awake."

Foxglove's voice. What was Foxglove doing here? Emmazel blinked but still couldn't get her eyes to work.

"Where am I?"

"After you fell unconscious, everyone agreed it would be best to bring you home. But you're not in the tower. This is a house Father owns in the village."

"Father owns a house in Hightower?"

"I know. It surprised me, too, but you know he had to have somewhere he was going when he was away. It's a nice place, not large, but nice enough. You'll be happy here, Emmazel." Foxglove took a deep breath. "We've already moved your garden to the backyard for you."

"Why can't I see anything?"

An edge entered Foxglove's voice. "I don't know. Maybe it has something to do with the fact that you tried to kill my daughter three days ago."

Emmazel fell back against the pillow as the memory of that *horrible* power struggle rushed through her.

"I'm sorry. Elin tells me to not hold it against you – that it was all just a natural response to the pain of your life and the recent changes, and that she pushed you too hard, but all I can think of is that I nearly lost both her and her sister, five years ago." Foxglove took another deep breath. This one sounded like a suppressed sob. "She told me to come and get her as soon as you woke. She wants to talk to you before she takes Earnest and the children back to the Forest."

Emmazel heard a door open and close, and she was left alone.

Her sight was gone, and she couldn't hear the world the way she was used to. What had happened?

The door opened and closed again. Footsteps. The creak of a chair. Someone took Emmazel's hand, and the world felt slightly more clear.

"I didn't want to do this to you, but it was the only way to detangle our magic once you took it to that point." Elinrose's voice was as matter-as-fact as always. "It was your sight or your memories, and I didn't want you to live the way my mother did. The recovery should be easier. You get to stay yourself."

"You want me to live with what I did." Emmazel stared sightlessly up at the ceiling.

Elinrose sighed. "I don't hold our fight against you. We were both stressed and upset, and it was my decision to begin the engagement. I knew how fast the battle could turn – after all, I used similar tactics to fight the Mistress. Maybe I was overconfident. Maybe I overreached. For that, I apologize."

"Stop piling responsibility on yourself." Emmazel shook her head. "I know I'm at fault. I'm not sorry, but I don't need you to work yourself up over me. You won. The Forest is yours. That's the end of it. Maybe I'm stronger, but how am I to compete against you *and* Earnest?"

"I told him to only interfere if he had to. I should have had him interfere sooner. I should have broken it myself when I realized that you wanted a *real* fight…"

"I told you. Stop claiming responsibility for everything. It's over and done, and it won't change anything."

Elinrose squeezed Emmazel's hand. "I don't think I know what to do with myself if I'm not taking responsibility for everything. Mari begs me to give it up, but old habits die hard."

"Night keeps telling me to stop meddling in the love lives of my companions, but I've been unable to give it up, either." Emmazel gave a dry laugh. "I like to think that I'm getting better. Haven't even used a love potion since I botched things so badly with your husband."

"I am ... still not sure what to think of the fact that you gave my husband a love potion."

"Well, it was harmless." Emmazel sighed and closed her eyes. "She's moved on, and that seems to be progressing well. Or, it was until three days ago. Do you think I might have ruined things for her?"

"I think that Heather is a bright, beautiful girl who will be able to get whatever unmarried young man she wants."

"Emphasis on unmarried."

"Most certainly."

"I'll get better about vetting potential suitors – that'll be the first question I'll ask from now on," said Emmazel. "Hello, sir, are you married? Yes? Well then, you're not who I'm looking for.'"

"Emmazel, I am going to return to the Forest soon." Elinrose's voice was all business again. "That fight left both of us drained, and it's been trying to pull me back ever since. I've fought the pull until now, as I've needed to talk to you, but not even Earnest will anchor me for much longer."

"Take care of it, then." Emmazel balled her free hand into a fist. "You've won it twice over now. I'll stay here and keep making potions."

"It was never about winning, Emmazel."

"I know, Elin. I've seen inside your head. I shouldn't have tried to take it all from you."

"I want you to know that I do hope to see you again." Elinrose's hand pulled out of Emmazel's. "And since I don't know if I'll ever be able to leave the Forest again, consider it an open invitation. It was supposed to be your birthright, and

I want it to one day be your home. I still want you as an ally. You're still family."

Emmazel gave a weak smile. "Do you think I could say good-bye to my namesake before you take her away?"

"I can get her," said Elinrose, and Emmazel heard her leave the room.

She'd lost. She'd tried to fight her niece, and she'd lost. Emmazel didn't know what she regretted most. Probably the fact that she'd completely lost her head. The palace had been completely the wrong place for the confrontation.

Slowly, carefully, she sat up, rubbing away a headache that suddenly throbbed in her temples. Then she froze as she realized how light and unhampered her head was. Her hair – her hand went to the back of her neck – what had happened to her hair! It barely grazed her shoulders in jagged ends.

"I'm so sorry about your hair." Elinrose's voice came from the doorway. "The power transfer causes certain physical changes. I don't know if you ever guessed this, but I didn't always have a rose vine growing out of my head. Well, you had begun the transformation before Earnest interrupted, and it's left a few scars. We salvaged what we could of your hair, but, well … it'll grow back?"

"I've never cut my hair." Emmazel shook her head. "That was forty-six years of growth!"

Elinrose sighed. "I did ask you to stop before we got to that point. Given that *I* would have died if you had won, I think you got off easy."

"At least I can't see how bad it is." Emmazel dropped her hand to her lap. "Small comfort there. You have Ela?"

"Yes, I do." Elinrose walked across the room, sat on the bed next to Emmazel, and slid Ela into Emmazel's arms. "There you go."

Emmazel took a deep breath as she adjusted to the weight in her arms. "I am sorry that I tried to take you from your family. Ela is going to need her mother. A good mother. It's just … where does this leave me?"

"Are you ready, Elin?" came Earnest's voice.

Elinrose stood and took Ela from Emmazel's arm. "I'm afraid you're the only one who can answer that question. Give it time." Then she pressed a kiss to Emmazel's forehead. Warmth spread through Emmazel's chest, and the silence was suddenly less oppressive.

"That was the last of my reserves," said Elinrose, exhaustion now threaded through her voice. "The Forest will restore me in a moment, and I don't want to leave you completely bereft."

Emmazel's breath caught as she pressed a hand to her heart. "Thank you. Really. I will recognize that you didn't have to do that. And since I've lived my life with my power strangled by the tower, I'll do all right. It'll be easier to sell my potions now that I live in town. I might not even need to depend on market day. I—" She cut herself off as she realized she wasn't being answered. "Elin? Are you already gone?" She hadn't heard them go – but there was an uneasiness to the room's energy, as though something had been displaced.

Had they vanished into thin air?

~

Emmazel fell back against the bed, choking back tears. Sight gone. Hair gone. She'd made a fool of herself in the palace. What else could go wrong?

"So, you're finally awake."

Her breath caught at Night's voice. He was at the foot of her bed. He sounded … upset.

"I'm sorry. I lost my head."

"Your father is distraught because of what you did. I honestly didn't think he would survive the night. What were you thinking, Emmazel!"

Emmazel's heart sank straight to her toes. "I wasn't thinking. That's just it."

"Your father has a lot of fears, but that you would turn out just like your mother has always been the greatest one. She knew where you were; as long as you stayed in your tower, she would have left you alone. But if you wound up just like her, welll!"

"I'm not like her!" Emmazel flew to her feet and whirled to face the direction of Night's voice. "I care about the people around me! I'm not cruel! I'm not heartless!"

"She used to care too, once. But her heart was broken, piece by piece, until nothing remained but a thirst for power."

"But that's not going to happen to me. I have you, Night." Silence.

"Night, please. You know I would never—"

"No, I don't know. What I know is that your mother was a monster, and you nearly killed your own niece three days ago because you couldn't stand the fact that she was more powerful than you."

"It wasn't about the power, Night!"

But that tasted like a lie, and she knew it.

"I shouldn't have stayed here so long," muttered Night, ignoring her. "I've always known better than to accept anything from your kind. I only stayed so long so I could stay close to – because your father said that proximity to you would help me – it was your father's idea, and no matter how in your own head you might be, you always did have good intentions."

"It was a mistake in the heat of the moment. Elin doesn't hold it against me. We talked it out. We're good now!"

"But do you still hold it against her?" asked Night. "I was sitting here, listening. You *hardly* apologized. It still rankles that she's the Gardener and you're blind."

"You expect me to be happy about the loss of my vision?"

"You can only blame yourself for it."

"I know that. I accept that – I do. Oh, Night, please believe me. Elinrose is the Gardener, and that's fine! She's a good Gardener. So much better than I can ever be."

"So much resentment still hides in your words, but I'm glad to hear that you finally use her name. Emmazel, your niece has been nothing but kind and gracious to you since she arrived. She's never once treated you as her enemy, even though you were the one person who had the power to destroy her. She wanted you at her side, but, no, you had to engage in that stupid fight and try to drain her of her magic. You knew that it would kill her, and you knew that her death would only hurt the people you cared about. It was horrid. Horrid, Emma! I can't even stand the sight of you right now."

"How bad are the scars?"

"Oh? So that's it? You're just going to laugh and make fun? You should be glad you can't see in the mirror, but it's not about the scars, or your hair. It's ... I can't do this anymore."

"What?"

"I can't keep sitting here, watching you wreck lives and dodge consequences." She heard him jump down onto the floor. "I'm tired of this torture of a life. Good-bye."

"Night, wait!"

"No, my mind is made up. There's nothing you can say. I have to go."

"Night! Night! Please, Night!"

But there was no answer, even as she shouted his name again and again. It was pointless, and soon she sank to the floor, no longer bothering to hold back the tears.

"Emmazel? What's wrong? Why are you calling for Night?" Heather's voice.

"He's gone," choked Emmazel. "He's actually gone."

27 The first thing she did was make right with her father. No one knew how much time they had left with him, so as soon as Emmazel's tears were dry, she asked Heather to escort her to her father's room.

He was asleep when she got there, but she sat at his side and took his hand to wait. The air was restless around him. It wasn't too late.

"Emmazel, is that you, child?"

She tightened her grip on his hand as she heard his voice. "It's me," she whispered. "I'm awake again. I … I survived my stupidity."

And it all spilled out. Everything she had been too afraid to tell him. All of her pain and confusion and fears. He held quiet through it all, his grip on her hand and the shifting of the air around them telling that he was still awake and listening.

"I know none of this is what you want to hear," she finally concluded. "I must be such a disappointment to you, and after everything you've done and given up to protect me!"

"Oh, Emmazel." Father gave a long, tired sigh. "No, none of that is what I wanted to hear, but what hurts most is that I never gave you the security to say any of it. I made you too afraid. How might things have been different if there had just been honesty between us? Had I told you *why* you had to stay in the tower instead of filling you with irrational fear?"

"You did the best you could."

"I keep trying to tell myself that, but did I? Or could there have been something, anything I could have done to avoid winding up here?"

"I'm sorry. I know you never wanted me to end up like my mother, but here we are." Emmazel forced a smile. "But it's not too late. I'm going to get better, I promise. You don't have to worry about me."

"Your mother's problem was that she didn't know how to be happy," said her father. "She was never content with what she had. And in trying to teach you contentment, I only taught you to fear the world."

"After the way she hurt you, it's amazing that you were able to see any good in me at all." She shook her head. "There were fragments of mother's memories in Elinrose's, when we were fighting. I think Elin showed them to me on purpose in an attempt to get me to back down."

Father gave another long sigh. "I tried to love your mother. I married her, after all. I gave it my best. And we had two beautiful daughters. But I don't think either of us really understood *how* to love. Her choice of me as her consort was never anything more than surface attraction and the fact that no one else was desperate enough to have her. I mean, what petty thief wouldn't leap at a chance to become a king? I was even able to get my sister out of that life and see her married to a good man. But I couldn't keep looking the other way, and as your power grew, your mother grew paranoid. So I took you away and promised you would never return to the Forest if she left you alone. I was going to keep that promise, too."

"You were going to keep me in that tower forever?"

"If I had to. If I could. You were safe." Father coughed. "I think, if I had ever thought you would be a match for your mother, and if I thought you would be an improvement over her, I would have told you. I would have let the choice be yours."

"And which was it? Was I never strong enough, or was I

never good enough?" Emmazel swallowed. Hard.

"You don't want me to answer that, Emma." He gave her hand an extra squeeze. "Because the truth is, I didn't trust myself to raise a daughter capable of facing Ferna."

Emmazel winced as she heard him say her mother's name.

"That's why I always made sure you had a companion. Why I convinced Night to stay and encouraged Berry to visit. But I never thought any of it was enough. Then it was pointless."

"Because the Forest found Elinrose instead."

"Yes. So all that remained then was to keep my promise and keep you in that tower and out of her way. I didn't know who the new Mistress might be, and I could only assume she would see you as a threat. When Earnest came looking for you, that was all of my worst nightmares come true."

"Night's gone, Father. He left, and I don't think he plans to return."

"Has he?" Father's hand twitched. "Well, he keeps claiming he'll do it and never carrying through. Was starting to get ridiculous about it, if you ask me. I'm glad he's finally made up his mind – or has he? Just because he left doesn't mean he can't come back."

"Maybe, but I think he really means to leave us." Emmazel frowned. "What I did has really upset him."

"Emmazel, your mother destroyed his life, and he's harbored that pain for a long time. And it upsets him when you remind him of your mother."

Emmazel hung her head. "And engaging in that fight with Elinrose … reminded him of her."

"He watched you try to drain the very life out of your own niece," said Father. "Family is important to him, and he really thought you were better than that. He was always the one to encourage me to see the best in you and to let you test your boundaries."

"Really?" Emmazel frowned. It was true that Night often argued in her favor, but he also never missed an opportunity to critique her. Infuriating cat.

"He seldom spoke ill of you behind your back, but he

reserved the right to bring your faults to your own attention. Had to keep you on the straight and narrow, just to be sure, you know." Father gave a weak laugh. "And it's helped him keep his mind for all these years. Poor Night! Losing his faith in you, well! It really would destroy him. No wonder he left."

"I'm sorry, Father." Emmazel leaned forward and pressed the back of his hand to her cheek. "It's been one mistake after another for me, hasn't it?"

"Well, that's what happens when people leave their towers, my dear. They make mistakes, get hurt, and disappoint the people they love. But they also forge new friendships, learn new things, and live life. I think you're going to do just fine, my dear. Just … make good with your sister, before she runs off like Night did. I've tried to talk to her, and so did Elinrose, but … she's a good mother. Someone did right with her, but it was neither Ferna nor I." He pulled his hand free and patted Emmazel on the cheek. "She raised a good daughter, and I hope I'll get to meet the other one, too."

"I hope so, too. She's the Frost. You should like her, since she shares your magic."

"I think I will. But Elin says she's emotional and still not quite over their father's death. Poor girl. She also has duties as the wife of Farra's crown prince. Now, let me rest, dear. And take care of yourself. Whatever mistakes you've made, you still have your life, and you can rebuild."

"I'll try not to disappoint you."

Emmazel carefully stood and felt her way out of the room. It was only a dozen or so steps to the door, and she found the door easily enough without knocking anything over.

"He's not going to hold grudges against you," said Heather, her hand slipping into Emmazel's. "You've said it yourself. He spoils you."

"I know. He's just going to blame himself for all of my mistakes." Emmazel scrunched up her face in a frown. "Elin must get it from him."

"Elin? Not Mrs. E anymore?" Heather jostled Emmazel playfully.

"We shared memories. Calling her by a derogatory nickname isn't appropriate anymore. And, really, it never was in the first place." Emmazel took a deep breath. "Could you take me to my sister? I need to apologize to her."

"I'm here." Foxglove's voice came from across the room. "And I'm not going to hold that grudge, either. Much as I want to, you are my baby sister that I've worried over for so long. Elin says you latched onto her lingering resentment towards the Forest and acted on it."

"She wanted to make a point that she was just as trapped in the situation as I've ever been, but my agitation read it as a desire to escape responsibility. Heather, where can I sit down?"

"Oh, yes, of course." Heather guided Emmazel to an armchair.

"Elinrose escaping responsibility seems like a fib, I know," said Foxglove. "Especially when you consider how she throws herself into it now. But she misses home, I know. It's been hard on her, though she never complains."

"But there's nothing anyone can do about it now." Emmazel leaned back and covered her eyes. "And it's been good for James that he hasn't had her as a crutch."

"Oh, it has been." Foxglove gave a tired laugh. "He's a good young man. Does his father proud. Still, if only I had been able to face Mother thirty years ago…"

Emmazel sighed. "You don't need to blame yourself for Elinrose's situation, either, Foxglove. Your weakness meant that you were able to meet her father, remember? If you had been strong enough to take the Forest from our Mother, then she wouldn't exist, nor would Snowmari. And I can tell you from experience that Elinrose is rather fond of existing."

"I—" Foxglove broke off with a sigh. "You're right. She tells me that all the time. But it's a mother's job to want the best for her daughters, you know."

"A good mother, that is."

"A bad mother doesn't do her job."

"True enough."

"I should fix dinner," said Heather, and Emmazel heard her

hurry away.

"You know, Father said that he was a thief before marrying our mother," she said after a minute. "He's never told me how he was able to provide for me all these years. Do you think…"

"I think that may be a question we don't want to have answered," said Foxglove.

"I think you may be right."

~

Their lives found a quiet rhythm after that. Emmazel slowly adjusted to the loss of her eyes and complained as little as possible. She took to spending most of her time outside in her garden, under the warmth of the sun. It hurt that her plants were once again as quiet as they had been in the tower, but it was enough. She could still tend them, and their voices helped her navigate the world.

A week passed quietly. Foxglove accompanied them to market, and their potions sold well. Some people asked about Emmazel's cut hair and lost sight, but Heather and Foxglove expertly deflected them.

No one discussed what the future would hold. Heather's romance couldn't progress with the man of her dreams so far away, and Foxglove and Emmazel were avoiding the reality of their father's mortality. They all just took it one day at a time, going about their routines and appreciating what they had.

And they had so much. They had their lives. They had love. They had the warm sun overhead and their freedom.

Emmazel stood in her garden, breathing deep the rich scent of earth and the myriad of aromas from her plants. It was a good day. A very good day – and nothing could ruin it because she was not going to make any foolish decisions. She was getting good at not making foolish decisions. She hadn't made any in a whole week. Granted, she had slept through the first three days and had failed to convince Night to stay, but failures weren't mistakes.

Her fingers grazed the bark of the hazel sapling that Elinrose had left behind. It was young still, but its connection to the Forest was strong. One day, it told her. One day. The Gardener waited.

"Emmazel!" Anna's voice broke into her thoughts. "Heather says that you're out here. Oh, but this is a nice garden you have now; so much better than your old one. Gardens just don't belong at the tops of towers, you know!"

Emmazel jumped up and spun around. "Anna! It's good to hear you."

"But not see me, eh?" Anna answered. "Heather already told me about your eyes. Such a shame! And your hair, too. You were so proud of that braid of yours – never was cut."

"Until now." Emmazel tossed her head back and shrugged. "But I'm alive, and I didn't kill my niece in a fit of anger, so I'll count my blessings."

"And when you consider how you looked a week ago, when you collapsed after that fight…" Anna gave a long sigh. "I always knew that you would land on your feet in the end, but, I suppose, one can't land until they hit the very bottom, now can they?"

"And I most certainly hit the very bottom." Emmazel gave a self-deprecating laugh. "I've learned my lesson. I'll find my own place."

"Oh, but here I am with only more bad news for you!" Anna took Emmazel's hand. "I am determined to tell you myself instead of letting you hear the official report tomorrow. If you ask me, Christian should be the one here to tell you, but his parents are unlikely to let him come this way any time soon, especially not to see you."

Emmazel squeezed Anna's hand. "What happened? Is he all right? Oh, I offended his parents, didn't I? I made such a fool of myself, and I haven't the faintest clue how to fix it!"

"Oh, dear child." Anna squeezed her hand back. "He's marrying Kendra Flaxseed."

Emmazel pulled back. "What?"

"I know – it was such a shock to everyone. They're claiming that you made the match, but Christian confided in Westbrook and me that they've been secretly engaged for months. Months,

Emmazel!"

"Really?" Emmazel frowned. "But that would mean that they were engaged ever since … since before…"

"Before you even left your tower, yes," Anna confirmed. "They met at Lord Dickon and Lady Camilla's wedding but didn't know who each other was until they were half in love already. They agreed that neither of their parents would approve the match, so they hatched a plan to make it appear that it was your doing."

"And they thought that their parents would accept *that*?"

"His parents, at least," said Anna. "You have quite a reputation in court, Emmazel. Noblemen who find wives from you have happy marriages – it's quite a fashion, really."

"I thought I was just that good," Emmazel mused.

"Oh, you are!" Anna pulled Emmazel close again. "But are you all right? I expected you to be so much more distressed by the news."

"Why should I be?" Emmazel frowned. "I mean, I am a bit put out that they would give me the credit without at least consulting me, but far be it from me to stand in the way of true love."

"But I was sure that he was here to court you! And the two of you got along so well! You've said so often that if he were to come to your tower, you would be tempted…"

"Yes, tempted." Emmazel shook her head. "And I was, at first – he's a very charming man. But I quickly realized that his life isn't the life I wanted to live. No, my heart remains my own, and I'm just confused that they would hide it so completely. He really seemed to despise her, and she, well, she was Kendra Flaxseed. Politeness and disappointed frowns. I did know that something was bothering her, involving a disagreement with her parents, but a secret romance? I never would have guessed that."

"Oh, but Westbrook and I had such hopes! Not to disparage Kendra, for he's chosen well for himself, and we are going to give them our full support to satisfy *her* parents. We're hurt that they wouldn't confide in us sooner, and after we had gone to such lengths to make the match for you! Are you sure you're fine? Because the two of you made *such* a lovely couple on the dance floor, and I was saving the news that Westbrook and I are expecting our firstborn in about seven months' time to make you feel better!"

"Oh! Congratulations for that!" Emmazel broke into a smile. "Anna, I'm fine. I have spent the last twenty-five years wooing suitors for my companions, and at the end of it all, Christian was just another suitor. I'll never marry – I've told you so before, and it remains true. In fact, I had already dismissed all thoughts of romance myself by the next morning, and – oh, Heather! This *can't* have happened to her again!"

# 28

After Anna left, Emmazel paced the garden for several minutes to gather her thoughts. Oh, that Kendra had only confided their dilemma from the start! Then Heather's heartbreak would have been over as soon as she discovered Christian's identity!

How had she not seen this? How had they hidden this so completely? Especially when they wanted *her* to take credit for it? How had she twice now tried to match Heather with a gentleman already belonging to another? The poor girl! If Emmazel had been superstitious, she would say that the girl had been born under an unlucky star.

There was nothing for it. Delays would make it harder. Emmazel turned her footsteps towards the house and marched inside.

It was getting easier to navigate without her eyes. She was memorizing the location of things and quickly learning to rely on her other senses. It was slow, but her confidence grew each day.

Still, she called for Heather as she crossed the threshold. It was so much harder to seek things without her eyes and pointless to check every room.

"I'm here!" Heather called back, and after a clatter of footsteps, her hand folded around Emmazel's. "Oh, Emmazel, is everything all right? You seem upset. What did Anna say? She only told me about the baby and Kendra marrying the prince. Strange news, to be certain, since they acted like they couldn't stand each other, but I'm happy for them if that's what they want."

Emmazel stiffened, her frown turning to confusion. "But what about you?"

"Me?"

"Yes! You!" Emmzel squeezed Heather's hand. "You had your heart fixed on him, and I encouraged you. Oh, I *should* have used a love potion on him, to be certain, but it all seemed to be going along so well, I didn't think it was necessary!"

"Wait—" Heather pulled back, sounding equally confused. "Why would I have any romantic interest in the crown prince? I already made that mistake with Earnest. I'm not meant for royal life, and princes can do so much better than myself."

"Oh, Heather, don't be so hard on yourself – any prince would be lucky to have you." Emmazel shook her head. "But what do you mean? You're in love! You told me so! What happened to your gratitude for the great service he did you?"

"You thought that I meant Prince Christian?" Heather pulled out of Emmazel's grip entirely. "You … you thought I meant Prince Christian! Oh, Emmazel!"

"He *rescued* you!" Emmazel lifted her hands in confusion. "Who else could you be talking about?"

"I … I meant Night! The way he sat with me the whole night, talking to me so I wouldn't be scared."

"Night's a cat!"

"A talking cat!"

"You can't marry a cat!"

"I can if he's a man under a curse and I break that curse with my love!"

"What?" Emmazel took a step back. "That's ridiculous! Night is a cat. The most irritating cat in existence, but a cat all the same. He—" Her breath caught. "He's just a cat."

"A cat who talks! Earnest told me about how *he* used to be a frog, and his brother was a bear. That's what the Mistress did.

Night has to be under a similar curse – and it can be broken by true love, just like it was for them. Although…” Heather’s voice turned thoughtful. “It didn’t work out for Earnest and Lilly, really. She actually loved a doctor, and he let her marry him. But that doesn’t mean that things will go badly for Night and me. I love him!”

“How could Night be a man? He’s a cat!”

How could a man in the form of a cat live in her tower for twenty-three years, and Emmazel not notice? Night was Night!

“You really never guessed?” Heather sighed. “Well, I suppose you’ve always just known him as a talking cat, Earnest didn’t come with his story until recently, and you’ve been distracted. But Night didn’t say no when I asked him if he was a man, so I really think he is.”

“And he can’t say it because it would take away his ability to talk,” mused Emmazel. “In the carriage ride to Boxill, he did say that most of the men my mother forced into the form of beasts have long-since lost their humanity. And he also said … I think he was *trying* to say that he was able to keep his humanity because he lived with me. But then he also said that love had little to do with Barend’s and Earnest’s disenchantments, and it was more the fact that Lilly and Elinrose are Sensitives.”

“Well, so am I,” said Heather. “That’s not a problem.”

“Do … do you have any idea if he might love you back?” Emmazel asked as she continued to reconsider everything that Night had ever said to her. And that she had said to him. If he was actually a man, what all did that change?

“Oh, I think he does,” Heather declared. “He’s always asking about me and my life. When we were picking strawberries, he even asked if I had any romantic prospects after things went so wrong with Earnest and Farmer Marrin. I didn’t know how to answer, but I told him I was completely recovered from both.”

Emmazel swallowed. “Well, I think he would be the last to intentionally lead you on, but … he’s a cat.”

“A cat who used to be a man and could be again,” Heather countered. “I don’t know exactly how to break the curse, but when he comes back, I'll find a way. I *promise*."

"If he comes back," said Emmazel.

"What?"

Emmazel pressed a hand to her head. "I'm sorry, but I … he didn't sound like he planned to come back, when he left. I think he's … he's going to give up. Stop fighting for his humanity."

"But – no. He can't! He'll come back! He has to!" Heather's voice trembled. "He just has to think for a while and remember! I have to go finish dinner."

With that, she scampered away, leaving Emmazel behind, her world spinning. Somehow she stumbled to an armchair and sat down, gripping her head.

Night had been a man. The one dependable constant in her life, for the last twenty-three years, and she had misunderstood him so fundamentally. Twenty-three years, a man had lived in her home, and she had treated him like a pet.

And what would her life be without him? She'd been avoiding that question ever since he'd left, unable to fully accept that he wouldn't be back, but would this be worse? To have Night return, only in a strange form and devoted to Heather?

But wouldn't she want him to be happy? If he would be happier in a human form, married to Heather, Emmazel should be happy for them. She wanted Night to be happy, certainly, but…

She wanted him to be happy with her.

She *was* jealous.

The thought caught, nearly choking her. She couldn't imagine her life without Night, especially not a life without her father, either. And both loomed over her.

Was this love?

It didn't feel like the right word. Or, at least, it was wrong if she used it the way she had for the last twenty-five years, as she matched her companions with nobles. There was no rush of attraction or romance, just the sense that if she never saw him again, it would be the air snatched from her lungs, and seeing him with someone else would be a knife in her heart.

He was a cat. She had always known him as such, and one couldn't see a cat as a potential husband – unless they were Heather, apparently. But Night, in the form of a man, well … that was another thing entirely.

She shouldn't think of it. She had ruined his opinion of her. Even if he did return, it wouldn't be the same as it had been. And if Heather could make him happy – well, Heather deserved a happy ending more than anyone Emmazel knew.

Emmazel deserved that knife in her heart.

~

One night of tears later and Emmazel was ready to face the world again. There was no dwelling on what she couldn't change, and the most logical step was more apologies – specifically, apologies to Kendra Flaxseed, who she had so terribly misunderstood.

Heather accompanied her, while Foxglove stayed home with Father. Silence hung heavy between them as both were occupied by thoughts of a certain black cat who might or might not have once been a man.

They didn't know if they would be welcome at the Flaxseed estate. Emmazel had apparently matched their daughter with the family's political enemy – would they want her to be a continued influence?

"Oh! Oh! Emmazel! It's you! You're here! Oh, I went to the tower to see you, but you weren't there, and I was so worried! But here you are, so that means you're all right. Why aren't you at your tower?"

Berry's voice was unmistakable as she flitted around Emmazel's head, and Emmazel smiled at the familiarity. "I live in the village now. The tower was just too inconvenient, and we found out my father had another house, so there we moved. Heather and I are here to see Kendra, if that's possible."

"Oh, Emmazel! I'm so sorry – she's in Boxill with the prince," answered Berry. "But she left a letter for you! I can get it!"

"Yes, please," said Emmazel.

"We probably should have assumed that Kendra wasn't home," said Heather. "After all, it was Anna who brought us the news."

"True," said Emmazel. "But it's the thought that counts, right?"

"Maybe," said Heather.

"And here it is!" Berry had returned and was flying around Emmazel's head with gusto. "Oh, this is so exciting! After all these years, she has written *you*! I *knew* that the two of you would be such friends!"

"Do you mind reading it for me?" asked Emmazel. "I injured my eyes last week and can't read anymore."

"Oh, you poor thing!" Berry cried. "Of course I shall! Just sit down! Oh, but this is so wonderful! I get to read you a letter that Kendra wrote especially for you! I thought this day would never come!"

Heather guided Emmazel to a seat, squeezing her hand, and Emmazel leaned back and closed her eyes. "So, what does Kendra have to say to me?"

There was a rustle of paper, and Berry cleared her throat.

"Dear Emmazel," she began, in an "important" voice. "I would like to thank you for your help in this matter. I will confess that I was skeptical of the plan at first, hence my reservation when we were together. I could also tell that you were quite distressed by the visit of your estranged relations, and I didn't want to burden you with my own struggles as well. However, all has turned out right for me now, and I hope your life will take a similar turn.

"I also hope that our friendship can proceed under different circumstances, but not in too near a future. Call me a jealous woman, but Christian was just a little too taken with you for my comfort.

"But I do wish you all the best of health and that you will someday find love yourself. Life is much better once you find where you belong, and while I have long-argued that a woman doesn't need a man for happiness, I suspect that you are one who truly desires marriage, even if you say otherwise.

"Austere be with you,

"Kendra Flaxseed, betrothed of the prince."

"Thank you," said Emmazel as she struggled to swallow down the lump that formed in her throat. "I'll try to find the means to write her back."

It stung to be so transparent, and yet it was freeing, too. As though tower walls were being torn down from around her heart.

**29** Two more weeks passed. Heather and Emmazel continued to not speak of Night. He was gone. There was nothing they could do about that. Father's health was a little worse each day. There was nothing they could do about that, either. Emmazel's magic grew stronger each day. Slowly. Surely. She didn't know if it would ever be enough to restore her vision, but it was something.

She wondered if the hazel tree might have something to do with it. Just in case, she spent extra time with it each day, and it was twice her height already. Soon, very soon. It was almost ready.

A few more words of encouragement and she moved on to her peppermint. An uneasiness filled the air. She frowned. Then there was a pop and the tension broke, but something still felt displaced.

"Emma."

Her breath caught. That was Night's voice.

No. No. She had to be hearing things. It was nothing but her wild imagination. And yet…

"You came back," she whispered.

"I did," he answered, proving his presence. "I heard the news and … I needed to be here for you."

"I thought…" The words caught in her throat, and tears

sprang to her eyes unbidden. "I thought…"

"Hey there." Night's voice was soft, and Emmazel felt a hand on her shoulder. A man's hand. She stiffened, choking on her tears. He was human. "It's going to be all right."

And even as she tried to fight it, as his arms folded around her, it just felt natural to bury her face in his shirt. He rubbed her back, muttering comforting words in her ear.

She wanted to stay in that moment forever. Held tight in his arms, not thinking of how or why he was a man again.

"Time will heal the wound," he muttered. "You didn't need that meddlesome prince, besides. You were always too good for him."

Emmazel pulled back, dashing her tears away. "What does Christian have to do with – I *made* that match." She swallowed. "Well, officially, I did. But you should know better than anyone. I *told* you I had no more interest in him than I had for any other gentleman who visited my tower, but you, you *stupid* cat, you wouldn't believe me!"

She fell back against his chest and drew in a shuddering breath as she fought to regain control of herself.

"Is it your father, then? I didn't even think of him." Night's arms tightened around her. "How is *he* doing? Is he…"

"He's worse each day but still hanging on," she answered. "I'm slowly accepting it, but grateful for the time I have left. Foxglove is usually with him these days. I have had him for the last forty years. She deserves the time he has left. And she's better-suited for nursing, besides."

"I'm glad you have this time."

Emmazel swallowed. "I didn't think you were going to come back. And, well, I still can't see you, but you're here. I didn't drive you to give up. Oh, Night, I didn't know what I was going to do without you."

Night tensed. "I'm so sorry, Emmazel. I regretted leaving you from the moment I was out the door. I should never have left the way I did. In anger. Not saying good-bye to anyone I cared about. Not a proper good-bye, at least. And when I think about the things I said to you!"

"I deserved every word of it."

"No. No, you did not." Night's hand cupped the back of her head. "Not when I was never angry at you at all, but only at myself for my weakness. And I am so sorry for staying away for so long, but I needed to think. And I didn't want to get in the way of your happiness."

"That's the most foolish thing I've ever heard you say." Emmazel frowned. "Silly cat. As though I could ever be happy without you."

Night went completely still, even so far as to stop breathing. "Emmazel," he said. "I'm not a cat anymore."

Emmazel's own breath caught again, and she forced a smile as she pulled back. "I … had noticed that, actually. Cats don't have hands."

He gave a low chuckle. "No, they don't."

Her smile eased as it turned genuine.

"Emmazel," he said. "There's something I need to tell you."

Her smile fell as her heart plunged straight to her toes. This was it, then. He had somehow already met with Heather, and her love had broken the curse. These stolen moments together in the garden had been just that. Stolen.

"I—" The words stuck in Emmazel's throat. With a sharp breath, she stood, turned away, and retreated, fighting to gain control of her unruly heart. It had been one thing to deny herself when his humanity had only been a vague idea, but when her head was filled with his scent and her heart still rested in his embrace, it was harder to quell her disquiet.

But he was her friend. Her dearest friend. And Heather, too. She owed them her support. She couldn't just walk away.

"Emmazel, what's the matter?" His hand closed around hers.

She squeezed his hand back. "Night, what if what you're about to say changes everything? What if we can't go back?"

"Everything has already changed," he answered. "We have to decide how to move forward."

"I can't risk your friendship." Emmazel took a deep breath and raised her chin. "I've been far from fair to you all too often.

Say what you must, and I promise to stand by you as your friend."

"As my friend?" Night gave a wry laugh as he turned her to face him. "Oh, Emmazel."

She swallowed and forced her smile back into place. "I'm here for you, Night."

Night took a deep breath, slid a hand around the back of her neck, and leaned down to press his forehead against hers. He was *tall*.

More than ever, she wished that she had her eyes so she might be able to see him.

"My name is Thomas Nighten," he began. "And before I was a cat, I was a common huntsman in your mother's Forest. I had a wife, Jana, and she was the light of my eyes and the center of my world. I loved her and would do anything for her. When the years passed without children, I did the unthinkable and went to your mother to bargain for a cure. She gave it to me, but at a heavy cost."

"You're married?" The words were thick in Emmazel's throat. What would this mean for her and Heather both? Was Heather only ever destined to fall for men already taken?

"I was." Night pulled back to take a long, shaky breath, and Emmazel took that moment to dive back into the hug. For his sake. From the way his arms folded around her, he needed it desperately.

"The Mistress demanded our firstborn in exchange for her help," Night finally continued. "And, fool that I was, I thought it a fair trade. What was one child when more would follow?" His voice rose in pitch as he spoke, so Emmazel laid her head against his shoulder and held him tighter. "But then the baby arrived, and the Mistress came to take her. Jana was devastated. I thought another baby would help, but more years passed without one. When we did have our second daughter, she only got worse. Would barely move. Hardly eat. I cared for them both as best I could, eventually taking the baby out with me when I hunted, but … I was helpless. One day, I came home to find Jana missing, and it was three days before I discovered her, dead at the bottom of a ravine. I don't … I don't know what happened, and I scarcely know what happened after that."

"It's not your fault," Emmazel muttered. "My mother never played fair."

"But I knew better, and I never cared about the cost until it was too late. And then … there was a place, near where I lived, a crack in the Mistress's defenses, which I later learned is what hid you from her. I was able to smuggle my daughter out of the Forest and leave her on the doorstep of a couple who I thought could give her the life I couldn't. I shouldn't … I should have stayed with her. Made the most of our newfound freedom and rebuilt, but no, I was a further fool who had to go and confront the Mistress. As though I could hold *her* accountable. As though that could fix a single piece of my broken life."

"And she turned you into a cat." Emmazel rubbed at his back. "I'm sorry. You didn't deserve any of that."

"I hadn't known I was a Sensitive – I knew Jana was, but the Mistress had already wiped out every other Sensitive man in the Forest. I should have suspected, given my ability to understand the animals I hunted, but it was safer to not know. And there are worse fates than life as a cat.

"I escaped through that gap again, and in retracing my steps, I found my way to your tower. Your father recognized me for what I was and invited me to live here. I didn't want to, for a multitude of reasons, but that first night, I heard you crying yourself to sleep, but you stopped when I let you hold me, and, I don't know … I felt like I had a purpose again. It kept me near my daughter, besides, allowing me to watch her grow up. Your father suggested that we move her to the tower, too, but I thought it best to leave her where she was. In hindsight … I don't know. Perhaps you would be more stable and mature if you'd had her to focus on. Perhaps she would have had a better life. Perhaps it would have made everything worse – and she's a far weaker Sensitive than you, so growing up in that tower … I didn't want to think about it then, and certainly not now. All

I know is that here we are now." Night took a deep breath as he ran a hand through Emmazel's hair. "I never thought that I would love again after I lost Jana, but *here I am*. This feels like a betrayal on so many levels, but I'm *here*."

Emmazel took a deep breath of her own. "And … I'm happy for you. Really. I'm sorry. I … I hope to meet your daughter one day."

"Emmazel." Night said her name like he was clinging to life itself. "I want you to know both of them. Oh, Emma, Emmazel, Emmazalea, do I have a chance? I know you've only ever known me as the black cat who criticizes your every move, and that I've made such terrible mistakes in love before, but can I still love you anyway?"

Emmazel pulled back, blinking furiously, though it would do nothing to clear her vision. "What?"

What about Heather? She'd broken his curse – hadn't she?

"Your fear was right." Night fidgeted with her hand. "I did leave you, intending to give up my humanity and forget it all, but I'm a stubborn man, and instead, I found myself in the Forest again, seeking the Gardener, to ask if she might know what had happened to my eldest daughter, if she still lived."

"Is she?" This was safe conversation … right?

"Oh, yes – Lilly." Night gave a small laugh. "I suspected, when Earnest mentioned her, but I wasn't sure that the Mistress would have kept her name. She's the Gardener's right hand, and I couldn't be prouder of her. She's the one who restored me to my human form – she insisted, since I wouldn't take the favor from the Gardener herself – and I've spent the last three weeks with her and her family. She's happy. All grown up."

Emmazel squeezed his hand back. "But you missed out on her life."

"I did. But at least Lilly found happiness in the end. And she helped break the Forest free from the Mistress." Night was pulling Emmazel closer again. "And she was very gracious of having a long-lost father moping about her house for nearly weeks, caught up with thoughts of you. The daughter of the woman who stole her from me.”

Emmazel frowned again. “I—”

“I don’t know how or why or when it happened, Emmazel,” Night continued. “And I still don’t know how it fits with my love for Jana. She was the light of my eyes, but you’re the very breath in my lungs. I don’t have the *words* to explain how much I love you. It’s too deep and true to explain. All I know is that you have kept me anchored for the last twenty-three years, and I don’t know how to live without you.”

“Oh, Night,” she breathed.

“Emma.”

“Don’t you ever leave me again.”

“Happily.”

Emmazel took deep breaths as the pieces of her life fell back into place. Night belonged with her. She belonged with him. The world was as simple as that. She lifted a hand to his cheek, feeling the stubble of a beard.

“What do you look like now?” she asked.

His grip of her tightened, and he pulled her closer. “The Gardener sent me back with something for you. Said it would be easier for the hazel tree to catch me if I had an extra share of magic, and you needed it besides. Can I kiss you? She said a kiss is the easiest way to give it to you, and I desperately want to kiss you, besides. But maybe it’s too soon…”

“Night, you’ve been with me for twenty-three years, and you’ve been my friend when I had no one else.” She slid her hand up his jawline, fingered the curl of his ear, and then tangled a fist into his hair. “This might be sudden, and it might be strange, but I’ve never been so sure of anything in my life. I would go down with you to the chapel and marry you this very second, if you asked.”

“Perhaps this afternoon.”

With that, his lips crushed against hers, and he kissed her with the desperation of a man dying. Her eyes slid closed as she savored it, and warmth spread through her chest as her senses sharpened.

It was over far too quickly, and Night pulled back, breathing hard. "Is that better?"

She gripped Night's shoulder as she centered herself among the voices of her plants, once again as loud as they'd ever been. When she opened her eyes …

The world was not as crisp or clear as it used to be – at a distance, colors blurred together into indistinction. But the man that was Night, looming over her, was clear enough, with sharp green eyes, golden hair, and the shadow of a beard she'd felt. There were lines about his eyes, telling of a man who laughed easily, but he didn't seem old. Weathered, yes, but not old. He wore a forest green outfit, and he gazed down at her with concern. Not quite the image she'd created of "Night-as-a-man," but she liked it. What was a face when it was the man she loved?

"The Gardener warned that your vision would probably never be what it once was," he continued. "But you should have most of your magic back."

"You're here," she whispered. "The world is perfect." With that, she pushed herself to her tiptoes and kissed him again.

~

"Is it all right if I continue to call you 'Night'?" Emmazel asked, laying her head against Night's shoulder. They had found a bench to sit on while they sorted through their mess of emotions. With words *and* more kissing, of course. "You've not said anything about it so far, but if you would prefer me to call you 'Thomas,' I can. It's just … I've always only known you as Night."

"Call me whatever you like, my dear," said Night, resting his cheek against the top of her head. "In many ways, the man who was Thomas Nighten died with Jana twenty-three years ago. I've been Night the cat for so long, I will proudly continue to answer to the name, especially from your lips."

"How old are you?"

Night gave a long sigh. "I was thirty-two when I lost everything, and I've been here with you for twenty-three years, but I don't think I aged a day while a cat."

"You're only nine years older than I am," Emmazel said. "And I only seem to be in my twenties, due to being a daughter of the Forest. It works out."

"Perfectly." Night pressed another kiss to her forehead.

"And you really thought that Prince Christian had stolen my heart?" Emmazel looked up to give him a saucy grin. "You were jealous!"

Night wiped away that grin with another kiss. "I was, perhaps, projecting my own insecurity, realizing that he had hands to do what I couldn't. You were free of the tower, everything had changed, and where did that leave me?"

"I would have kept you at my side, I promise."

"But watching you with another man would have been pure torture." Night caressed her cheek with his thumb. "I was a fool, you know. Earnest and Elinrose both offered to give me back my proper form, but I was too proud to accept help from either of them. Then I thought all hope was gone after our trip to Boxill, so I left, selfishly."

"I concur on that point. But I think we both needed time to think." Emmazel laid her head against his shoulder again.

"It was only when the Gardener visited Lilly this morning with news of Prince Christian's engagement that I realized I could act – and I knew I needed to be at your side. I honestly thought he had broken your heart."

"No, that honor belongs to you, when you left me." Emmazel pressed a kiss to his cheek. "You know, I never once guessed that you might actually be a man, in all these years. It was Heather who figured it out."

"Clever girl." A grin pulled at the corner of his mouth.

"But I knew, the moment I heard your voice again and felt your hands, my heart was yours, and there was no taking it back. How could I not love the one friend who has been with me for all these years?"

"How could I not love the girl who gave me purpose and showed me time and time again that it was possible to not just live, but *flourish,* even under the worst circumstances. Even if she might be the Mistress's daughter. Meddlesome you might be, but your intentions have always been good. And who am I to blame you for bad decisions when your world cracked into pieces?"

"I'm not my mother. And I hope to never again give you cause to see her in me."

Their lips met again for more kissing.

"Emmazel! Emmazel, I have the strangest news!"

Emmazel broke away from Night, a gasp catching in her throat at Heather's voice. Oh, *what* was she going to think? She'd had her heart fixed on him, and now this?

Night stood as eagerly as she did – though she doubted he would march to the house with such purpose if he knew Heather's declarations. How *did* he really feel about her? What had been the root of his interest in her?

Because there had been no romantic interest at all. Emmazel knew that as certainly as his grip on her own hand.

"I have strange news, too," she said as they found Heather standing in the house doorway. The girl was fidgeting with one of her braids, nervously shifting her weight from one foot to the other.

"Who's this?" Heather asked, noticing Night.

Night let go of Emmazel's hand, and Emmazel choked back a gasp of indignation. She had no reason to be jealous, right?

"My dear Heather," he said. "I am so happy to finally properly introduce myself. My name is Thomas Nighten, and I'm your father."

"Of course." The words spilled out of Emmazel in a breathless rush as every drop of jealousy evaporated. The child he'd left on a doorstep had been Heather. And that's why Lilly had seemed familiar in Elinrose's memories. She was Heather's sister.

"Night?" said Heather, taking a stumbling step towards them.

"Yes," said Emmazel, rushing forward to stand next to him. "He's home. And I'm sorry that this isn't what you wanted to hear, but he's a good man. You should be proud of him."

"Oh." Nervous laughter bubbled out of Heather. "That's

wonderful, really! Now everything makes sense! Emmazel, you see, I just met Farmer Marrin while on my walk, and he asked me to marry him again, and I said yes! He said that he'd been unable to put me out of his mind, even when he tried to court another girl, and that a black cat had encouraged him to ask again. And I realized that I'd only ever been comparing men to him. Emmazel, I'm sure I love him, and I was coming back to tell you that you would have to break Night's curse for me, because I couldn't. But here you are! It's all worked out so well."

"Yes, it has," said Emmazel. She glanced up at Night. "Heather thought your interest in her was romantic, and … well, you probably don't want to think about it."

"Given that it was her older sister who gave me back my proper form, romance wasn't necessary," said Night, tilting his head to the side, thoughtfully.

"I have a sister?"

"And I hope the two of you get to meet soon." Night took another step forward and pulled Heather into a hug. "I'm so sorry for not having been in your life the way I should have been – but I was determined to see you happily settled with a young man who would take care of you. And, if you want answers – you were born in the Forest, the Mistress took your older sister from us, and your mother died in her grief. I've done little but fail you your whole life, but I still love you so much, and I'm proud to be here in your life now."

"This is the happiest day of my life," said Heather.

Glancing up at Night as he pulled back to wrap his arm around her again, Emmazel quite agreed.

$\boldsymbol{30}$ Emmazel and Night were married that very afternoon, though in her father's room, so he could witness it. His presence was more important to them than any fuss or pomp, and they didn't know how much time they had left. And after twenty-three years of friendship, the ceremony felt almost superfluous.

Heather's wedding to Farmer Marrin was planned for the next spring and would be a much grander affair. It was nothing too fancy – the man was a farmer, after all – but Heather was happy, so Emmazel was happy for her.

Some days, she wondered what their lives would have been if different choices had been made. Who would she be if Night had never entered her life? Where would they be if she'd been brought Heather as a baby for her to raise? What might be different if she'd been raised as a true daughter of the Forest and had taken control of it some ten years before?

But the choices of yesterday had been made, and their life today was good. She woke every morning to the face of the man she loved best in the whole wide world, her very best friend and companion, and what more could she ask for?

Three weeks later, Father slipped into the Ever After in the middle of the night. Even though Emmazel had known this day was coming, Emmazel still cried the night away in Night's arms. No one said a word about it, least of all Night himself.

The funeral was a quiet affair, and Emmazel cried through it, too. Then it was time to decide what was to be the next chapter of their lives.

"You can return to your daughter now," Emmazel told Foxglove as she curled up on the sofa next to Night. "The hazel tree in the garden is ready, and there's nothing left to keep you here."

Foxglove nodded distantly, a small smile twisting her lips. "Elin left that tree for you, you know. She knew you were anchored here as long as Father lived, but she wants you in the Forest with her. She has plans. I have reservations, but she's the Gardener, not me. Despite everything, she trusts you. It's her right to do that."

"You raised a good daughter," said Emmazel.

"She takes after her father," said Foxglove. "He was a good man; I give him all the credit."

"We'll go in the morning," Emmazel decided, closing her eyes. Night's arms tightened around her, and he gave a contented sigh. "You don't mind staying and taking care of my garden for me, do you, Heather?"

"I can, yes," said Heather quickly.

"Just don't have your farmer over too often, dear," said Night, in his mock-stern voice, his hand playing in Emmazel's hair. "It's not spring yet."

"Right," said Heather, and Emmazel could *hear* her blushing. "How long do you plan to be gone?"

"It depends on Elinrose's plans and if Emmazel agrees with them," said Foxglove. "But there's a hazel tree in the garden, and you were born in the Forest. Your father will only ever be a wish away."

Morning came crisp and cool with the first winds of winter, and it was with great trepidation that Emmazel approached the hazel tree, her hand held tight in Night's. Foxglove led the way, disappearing first as she touched the tree's bark.

"Are you ready?" Night asked, pressing a kiss into her hair.

"I could run back into the house now," Emmazel muttered.

"I don't have to face her. You don't have to see the Forest again if you don't want to."

"That Forest holds more than enough good memories for me," Night answered. "I'm ready to make more of them. Don't use me as an excuse."

Emmazel gave Night's hand a tight squeeze before she let go and stepped towards the tree.

*I'm ready, Elinrose,* she whispered, as her fingers brushed the bark. The world shifted, and she stood in the Forest, standing in the clearing, next to Elinrose and Foxglove, who were pulling out of a hug.

Elinrose burst into a grin as she saw Emmazel. "You look well."

"I am well," Emmazel affirmed as Elinrose pulled her into a hug. "I'm … not the same woman you left in Howsill, two months ago, really I'm not."

"I wouldn't mistake you for her," said Elinrose. She gave Emmazel an extra squeeze and pulled back. "And, you're looking much better as well, Thomas Nighten. One would never guess you were the man I sent away last month."

"It feels like a lifetime ago," said Night, as his hand rested on Emmazel's shoulder. She glanced up at him with a smile. "And, please, just Night. My lovely Emmazel has declared that no other name will suit me, and thus it's the only one I'll use."

"Naturally," said Elinrose, a grin twisting her lips for a moment. "And my mother already told me, but I know what it means for you to have come. My condolences for your loss, Emmazel."

Emmazel gave a thin smile as she leaned into Night. "I still struggle to believe he's gone forever, but I'll keep going. It's what he wants me to do. And I don't blame you for his death anymore. I never should have. It was wrong of me."

"And now I know you are not the same woman I left two months ago," said Elinrose, her grin back in place.

"I'm not here to apologize," Emmazel continued. She glanced up at her husband. "I know it's what Night expects of me, but you don't want apologies, and I'll just make things more awkward between us as you try to brush it aside."

"Very true," said Elinrose. "Why waste words when actions speak louder? When we met, you were scared and confused at so many changes in your life, and I was happy to be the focus of your ire as you sought to find your center again. Even when it nearly cost me my life – which was *never* going to happen since Earnest was watching, though we came far closer to the brink than I liked. And now that you know who you are, I hope to call you friend."

"I hope to, as well." Emmazel swallowed and glanced towards Foxglove. "Your mother says that … you have plans concerning me."

"She calls it a plan. I call it a request." Elinrose sighed as she sat on a throne that grew out of the ground to catch her. "Emmazaela, would you bear the burden of the Forest with me?"

"What do you mean?" Emmazel straightened and took a step towards her niece.

"You know as well as I do that I never wanted to take this role," said Elinrose, pressing the heels of her hands to her temples. "I did what I had to, but it's not been easy. I wasn't meant for this role – I'm a strong Sensitive, but I wasn't born to inherit the Forest. *You were.* And I've done the best I can, but it's taking a toll on me. Frankly, I'm tired, and I can't even sleep."

"And you can't unbind from the Forest without dying," said Emmazel.

"I can, however, share the bond." Elinrose dropped her hands to her lap. "I've shared it with Earnest, of course, but he's barely a Sensitive at all – though more than I thought, it turns out. But … there is precedence for this. A pair of twins who couldn't decide who should inherit, so they shared the power. You're stronger than I am. Even after living in a tower for forty years and being drained in our fight, it's amazing. If we add your strength to this bond, it would be so *nice*. You were meant to bear the weight of the Forest, not me."

Emmazel stepped forward and took her niece's hand.

"What would it entail?"

Elinrose looked up with a smile, then leaned back and closed her eyes. "I would still be *the* Gardener; we wouldn't quite be equals. But you would command the Forest as I do, and we would both be free to travel, so long as one of us is here. If we are both here, then we can … we can take turns sleeping. Succession will probably pass through my line, but who knows? It could be yours. All I know is that it's not Ela. You will share my extended life, and so will your husband, both of you fading only after my death, as it was with your father. There are other things that may come up, but I don't know. Risks must be taken. I've been thinking on it for some time, but I've not yet been able to foresee everything."

"A while?" Emmazel tilted her head to the side. "Did you only ever seek me out to foist the power of the Forest upon me?"

Elinrose gave a small laugh. "I sought you out because you're family and I want to fix what the Mistress broke. The idea didn't even occur to me until we met in person for the first time, and there you sat, a shining beacon of power, and my own power was reaching back to you! The Forest wants you, Emmazel, though I wasn't going to say a word to you about it so long as your heart would be torn." She leaned back and held Emmazel's gaze. "And I can still hear you as clear as ever. You're of a mind to accept." She frowned. "A linking of our minds is also going to happen, but we won't be privy to *every* one of each others' thoughts, I promise."

Emmazel nodded. "I am of a mind, yes. But not for any reasons you might fear," she glanced back over her shoulder at Night and Foxglove. "You told me once that Austere had plans for us even in the messiest situations, and I believe you now. I would have been a terrible successor to my mother. The Forest needed a strong leader to heal it, and you were far more equipped in that matter than I ever could have been. But if you have need of my strength now, then I cannot refuse you, unless my husband should forbid me. I won't force anything on him, and it will concern him, too."

She retreated to Night and took his hand, staring up at him with a hesitant smile.

Night squeezed her hand and kissed her forehead. "I can forbid you nothing, my dear, and it will please me to walk these woods knowing that you'll be with me wherever I am, no matter the distance between us."

Emmazel turned back to Elinrose. "So how will this work? I expect you wish to do this at once."

"Neither one of us sees a point in delaying once our minds are made up," Elinrose agreed, standing, and her throne retreated back into the ground. She took Emmazel's hands. "To be honest, you already did half the work in our fight when you tried to take the power from me. I just have to reopen the link you forged between us – and there we go!"

Emmazel staggered as the weight of the Forest suddenly crushed upon her, a cacophony of voices far more distinct than she'd ever heard before. Elinrose pulled her closer, pressing their foreheads together as she sorted through it all.

"This is difficult, I know," she whispered, pressing her hands to the sides of Emmazel's head. "Clear your head, take a deep breath, and pick one thing to focus on. You'll get used to it eventually, but it's a lot, I know. I've already asked Ash to try to quiet the rest of the Wood Spirits, if she can. They're excited to have you, Emmazalea."

Emmazel took that deep breath and released it, holding on to Elinrose's voice like a line to the surface. *I'm excited to be here.*

*Good,* Elinrose answered. "And, thank you. I think we're going to work well together. Welcome home."

Emmazel took another deep breath and pulled back, testing the stability of her mind. "You're far more generous than I deserve. Any sane person would have turned me away and never looked back, after what I did."

"But I always knew your heart, though I'm probably going to get an earful from Mari next time she visits. Perhaps I should surprise her with a visit, first." Elinrose smiled at her. "The Forest looks good on you, by the way. You now have azalea growing out of your head. We make quite the pair."

Emmazel lifted a hand to her head, finding a cluster of flowers growing from behind her ear, and a smile spread across her face as she realized that her braid now hung to her waist again, leaves and flowers woven through it.

"Thank you."

"No, thank you." Elinrose laughed. "And congratulations, by the way."

"What?"

Elinrose raised an eyebrow as she directed Emmazel's focus.

"Oh," said Emmazel. "*Oh.*"

~

"Are you happy, my dear?"

Emmazel smiled as Night pulled the covers over them and then rested his hand against her middle. While the prospect of motherhood filled her with trepidation, she had taken a fertility potion their first night together, and Night's face when she told him of her pregnancy had made it all worth it. He deserved a second chance at fatherhood, and she still had seven months to adjust.

Everything would be *fine*.

Even if she was having twins.

"Quite," she said, laying her hand over his.

And she was. Her life was good. Learning to work with Elinrose this last month had been an adjustment, but they got along well and had proved remarkably like-minded. She had been happy to leave most of the politics to her more-experienced niece, but she shouldered whatever she could. Night, for his part, had quickly fallen back into his old life as a huntsman, and he'd been thrilled to build a home for them just down the road from his elder daughter. And Lilly had been more than happy to relinquish her role as Elinrose's right hand, ready to focus on her own growing family.

"There is one thing, though," she mused, rubbing her thumb against his. "It's ridiculous, really, but I ... I miss you."

"I'm here, dear," he muttered. "I'm not going anywhere."

"No, what I mean is … I know it's horrible, but I miss the cat you used to be. I mean, having you as a man is ever so much nicer, but … sometimes I miss having you curl up in my lap, purring into oblivion while I scratch you behind the ears."

"Ah." Night pulled his hand free of hers, resting it on her shoulder instead. "Emma."

Her breath caught as he didn't continue, and she rolled over to face him. His hand caught hers as she stared into his eyes. "What?"

"Emma, if you want me to be a cat, I can be a cat."

She frowned. "But you…"

"I know you like to call it a curse, but it wasn't. A cat is a natural form my body can take. I just don't have enough of my own power to make the shift myself. Earnest, perhaps could, but he seems disinterested in testing it, and I'm not bound to the Forest the same way he is, just to you."

"I see." Emmazel nodded slowly.

"I *liked* being a cat, really I did," he continued. "And I've missed it too. I only hated being trapped in that form."

"So, you're asking for some of my magic?" Emmazel arched an eyebrow.

"I'm saying that I would happily be a cat again for you if you'll lend me some." Night gave her a hopeful smile. "I only ask that you never force a shift on me in anger and never trap me in either form as a punishment."

"I'll agree to those terms, just make sure you never use your cat form to hide from fatherhood again." They sat up, and Emmazel pressed a kiss to his lips. "That should be enough for you to shift into a cat and then back into a man, when you're ready. Happy with that?"

Night gave her a contented half-grin; then, the next moment, he was the black cat she knew and loved. He turned in circles a few times, then settled on top of the covers beside her. She reached down and scratched him behind the ears, and soon he was purring loudly.

"Silly cat," she whispered.

More purring.

"I love you."

# Coming Soon...

## Snowfield Palace

When *The Snow Queen* invades *Mansfield Park*
Winter 2022

## Thornrose Estate

When *Northanger Abbey* discovers *Beauty and the Beast*
Summer 2023

## A Little Persuaded

When *The Little Mermaid* needs some *Persuasion*
Fall 2023

# Acknowledgements

Thanks so much to everyone who help me brainstorm and create this story! Again, especial thanks to Kelsey for encouraging the first spark when it came to me.

A huge thank you to everyone who's read and given me feedback, as I've written. Sarah, Patience, Rachel, Brielle, Cat, and a few others.

And thank you to you, lovely reader. I hope you enjoyed reading this story as much as I did writing it.

# About the Author

Kendra E. Ardnek is the penname of Kendra Roden, a Christian author who makes her home in the Piney Woods of East Texas with her herd of giraffes and clutch of dragon babies, alongside her honor guard of nutcracker figurines. When not writing, you can usually find her sitting in a box, because she might actually be a cat, and she's frequently been known to act before she thinks.